PUFFIN BOOKS

THE WHITE HORSE GANG

Sam Peach didn't expect to enjoy having his cousin Rose to stay for months on end. And he certainly didn't expect that his hero, Abe Tanner, would like her enough to give her his dead rats, but Rose was soon an indispensable member of the White Horse Gang. In fact, it was because Rose was so dreadfully homesick that the boys hatched their fearful plan of kidnapping little Percy Mountjoy, the cosseted mother's darling. They wanted to raise the money for Rose to go to America to see her parents.

Fortunately, somehow or other their shocking plot misfired, and they found themselves in danger of another kind, with real tragedy lurking round the corner.

This is another immensely readable story by the author of *The Peppermint Pig* and *Carrie's War*. For readers who like adventure with a good deal of suspense thrown in.

Nina Bawden spent her childhood in different parts of England. During wartime evacuation from London, she was sent to a mining valley and she also spent time in Norfolk in her grandmother's house, and in a farmhouse in Shropshire. Within a year of graduating from Somerville College, Oxford, with a degree in Philosophy, Politics and Economics, she had finished her first novel. Her houses and her experiences provide the real-life settings for her books and since the publication of her first children's book in 1963, she has had many books published, most of which have been adapted for film or television. She has also written several adult novels.

NINA BAWDEN

THE WHITE HORSE GANG

PUFFIN BOOKS

PUFFIN BOOKS

Published by the Penguin Group
Penguin Books Ltd, 27 Wrights Lane, London W8 5TZ, England
Penguin Books USA Inc., 375 Hudson Street, New York, New York 10014, USA
Penguin Books Australia Ltd, Ringwood, Victoria, Australia
Penguin Books Canada Ltd, 10 Alcorn Avenue, Toronto, Ontario, Canada M4V 3B2
Penguin Books (NZ) Ltd, 182–190 Wairau Road, Auckland 10, New Zealand

Penguin Books Ltd, Registered Offices: Harmondsworth, Middlesex, England

First published in Great Britain by Victor Gollancz 1966
First published in the United States by
J. B. Lippincott Company, Philadelphia and New York 1966
Published in Puffin Books 1972
13 15 17 19 20 18 16 14

Printed in England by Clays Ltd, St Ives plc
Set in Linotype Granjon

For all my friends in Shropshire,
especially for Jim

CHAPTER ONE

'HEY Mum, do you know what?'

No answer.

'Hey, Mum.'

No answer.

'MUM.'

Sam bellowed with the full force of his lungs. His face turned red as a plum.

'I'm not deaf, dear. There's no need to shout.'

Mrs Peach stopped cutting up steak for the dogs' dinner and looked at Sam in the kindly but somehow *unseeing* way she looked at most human beings most of the time. Though she was fond of Sam, she would really have been more interested in him if he had been a dog. Though Sam knew this, he did not resent it – indeed, from his point of view, the situation had its advantages. Other mothers fussed their sons about washing behind their ears and keeping the house tidy. Mrs Peach fussed over her salukis instead: she was too busy grooming them and getting burrs out of their coats to worry over such an unimportant thing as a bit of dirt on the back of a boy's neck. As a result, Sam confined his washing activities to as small an area as possible: if he washed his face he stopped short at his jaw line so that he often looked like a dark boy wearing a fair, freckled mask. Today he had omitted even this trifling attention. Looking at him in her abstracted way, Mrs Peach thought he looked exceptionally well and brown.

'What did you want, dear?' she asked.

'I can't remember now.'

'You must have wanted something.' Mrs Peach tried hard to be a conscientious mother. 'Are you hungry, dear?'

'Not specially. We've just had dinner,' Sam reminded her.

'Oh. Well. . . . Shouldn't you be getting back to school, then?'

'It's Saturday.'

'So it is. How silly of me. The vet came yesterday to look at Lady – he always calls on Fridays.' She regarded Sam with a perplexed expression. 'Saturday . . . I'm sure there was something I meant to do on Saturday . . .'

'Shopping? Eggs? Bacon? Baked Beans?' Sam spoke with an eye to his stomach. There was always plenty of dog meat and biscuits in the house but other things were liable to run short. 'Sunday joint? Vegetables?' There was no answering gleam in Mrs Peach's eye. 'Paying the milkman?' Sam suggested.

'He called this morning but I couldn't find my purse.'

'Behind the clock on the mantelpiece. If you'd asked me, I'd have told you.'

'You weren't here, or I would have done.' Mrs Peach ran her fingers through her short hair in the way she did when trying to remember something she had forgotten. (As she was always forgetting something, her hair was nearly as untidy as Sam's.) 'Oh well, perhaps I'll remember later,' she said, and sighed.

Sam shifted from one foot to the other. 'I'm going out.'

'Where you going?'

'Nowhere.'

'Give my regards to Mr Nobody, then,' Mrs Peach said, and then added, as Sam reached the door, 'I hope "nowhere" doesn't include Gibbet Wood.'

Sam held still for a moment; it struck him that for a vague, forgetful person, his mother often showed uncanny insight. In case he should need to lie, he crossed his fingers in his pocket, but it was all right, his mother just said placidly, 'I daresay they'll be out shooting this afternoon, as it's Saturday. I should hate it if someone shot you instead of a pheasant.'

That was all. Sam shot out before she could take it into her head to ask him a direct question. Not that he had actually intended to go to Gibbet Wood this afternoon – the idea scared him, though for other reasons than the chance of stopping a stray bullet from an amateur sportsman's gun – but the possibility was always at the back of his mind that he might, just might, get up the courage to go there someday, and he did not want to have to make any promises about it.

Now this danger had been averted, he began to wonder, idly, where he *should* go – not Gibbet Wood, not today – and while he made up his mind he began swallowing air, gulping at it in an attempt to achieve the one thing in the world he wanted to achieve at this moment which was a controlled belch as performed by Abe Tanner. Of all the boys in the town of Castle Stoke, Abe Tanner was the one Sam admired most and most longed to be admired by, and Abe Tanner could belch when he chose. When asked how, he said he didn't know, it was just something he could do. And, because Sam couldn't do it, it seemed the most desirable accomplishment he knew. But though he gulped and swallowed until he looked like a landed fish, he achieved nothing except a feeling of humility: he was cleverer than Abe Turner who was way behind him in spelling and arithmetic – though Abe was eleven, and two years older than Sam, they were in the same class at school – but he couldn't belch at will.

Sighing, he gave up the attempt, and wandered slowly down the hill, hands in pockets, limping hop-and-go-one in the gutter, and pretending he had an artificial leg.

The Peach house was halfway down the main street of the town, a long, thin street that curved steeply up the hill – too steep to bicycle up, but marvellous to free-wheel down – from the Castle Hotel and the church at the top, to the river and the football ground at the bottom. This street, River Street on the map, was referred to by the inhabitants as 'the Town'. The top of the street was 'up the Town', and the bottom, 'down the Town'. And, indeed, it *was* the Town: all the life of Castle Stoke went on there. Though there were back streets, they were very few and grass grew between the paving stones; most of the houses, as well as the five pubs, the four ironmonger's shops, the butcher's, the grocer's, the saddler's, the Post Office and the baker's, gave directly on to the narrow pavements of River Street and faced open country at the back.

Castle Stoke was a tired old town, Sam's father said. The weekly market was small and getting smaller, shops closed and no one took them over. The local farmers' wives went to the county town of Shrewsbury to shop nowadays, and where their women went, the farmers went too. Mr Peach, who kept the chemist's shop 'up the Town', between the Post Office and the Castle Bakery, said trade was bad and getting worse. Castle Stoke was dying on its feet, he said.

When he bothered to listen to his father, which wasn't often, Sam heard this with bewilderment. Castle Stoke always seemed to him to be full, brimming over with life. This warm afternoon, for example, walking down the Town he overheard at least six different conversations through the open windows. Among other things, Sam learned that Mrs Jones's daughter was having a new baby; that Doris Stretton was leaving home to work in a draper's shop in Aberystwyth; that Miss Marling was ill and going to have an operation. Miss Marling was still working, though. She was a dressmaker – there was a card in her window which said *Ladies' Reach-me-downs and Lingerie* – and her sewing machine was buzzing as busily as ever though the sound was less insistent and continuous than the evil whine of Mr Bason's dentist's drill. Mr Bason's surgery, in the front room of his house, had a horrid fascination for Sam who had recently had five fillings in his teeth. The bottom half of the sash window was shrouded by a net curtain, rather grey and holey, but not holey enough to see through. Sam stood on tiptoe to peer over it and see who was the current victim in the chair, but all he managed to see was the sideways view of the torturer himself, tall and stooped in his white coat. In his eagerness, Sam toppled over on his toes and rattled the window, which was loose in its frame. Mr Bason looked up, drill in hand and scowled ferociously. Sam hopped off, singing loudly to show Mr Bason he wasn't afraid of him.

Lower down, the street widened and was quiet. Like the pale, stubble fields, it lay peacefully slack in the September sun. An old dog slept on the flags outside the Three Tuns. It had been a long dry summer and, on the football field, the early fallen leaves lay crisply, looking as if someone had just spilled a giant cornflake packet. As Sam stepped on to the field, for no other reason than the pleasure of feeling the dry leaves round his bare ankles, he saw a small boy in a white shirt and white socks sitting on one of the benches. He was just sitting there, not doing anything; when Sam approached he stood up and smiled tentatively. Sam ignored him. He left the field and crossed the road. The small boy began to follow him. Sam increased his pace.

The boy's name was Percy Mountjoy and Sam loathed him, less on his own account than on his mother's. The Mountjoys were the only new people to settle in Castle Stoke in recent years. They had bought the old Bason house opposite the football field, a white, double-fronted house which had the distinction of being the only house on the street to boast a front garden, a narrow strip protected by an iron railing and an entrance flanked by two stone urns. When old Mr Bason, the dentist's father, had lived there, these urns had never contained anything except a skin of mossy growth on the sour earth, old cigarette packets and broken glass. Now they glowed with geraniums and the gleaming white paint on the front of the house put the rest of the town to shame. Or so Mr Peach said. In fact, Castle Stoke was not so easily shamed – it merely thought such pretty-ing up a terrible waste of good money – but it disliked the Mountjoys and not just because they were 'foreigners' from Birmingham. The Mountjoys were rich; this would not have mattered if they had not let everyone know it. They still owned a house in Birmingham in which Mr Mountjoy lived during the week, coming to Castle Stoke for weekends. Mrs Mountjoy went shopping in a fur coat and told everyone that they had only bought this 'funny little house' for Percy's health. There was nothing actually wrong with Percy, he was just delicate. It was a refinement of breeding rather than a failing. Percy was exceptionally sensitive. He was exceptionally talented. He was very musical – though as far as Castle Stoke knew, all he could play were a few tinkling pieces on the piano. But how could Castle Stoke judge such a paragon? Percy could not ride a horse but Mrs Mountjoy had been heard to say she was sure he would ride extremely well if he did. He was so good at everything and had a remarkable mathematical mind for a boy of seven. Perhaps he had, but no independent evidence was available as Percy did not go to school in Castle Stoke, but to a boarding school in the south of England, where he had a great many friends, Mrs Mountjoy said, some of them titled.

All this, or most of it, was said in front of Percy who always accompanied his mother when she went shopping, to carry her basket. (Percy had beautiful manners.) Sam, who had been in his father's shop when Mrs Mountjoy had been holding forth, thought he might have been a bit sorry for Percy if he had looked ashamed and hang-dog, or even the least bit restless. But he never did. He just stood, holding his mother's basket and looking impassive as a stone idol, even when Mrs Mountjoy suddenly whipped out her handkerchief and dabbed at his cheek to remove some invisible piece of dirt – just as if she were dusting a piece of furniture, Sam thought disgustedly.

It had embarrassed him to discover that Percy was anxious to be friends with him. One day, when Mrs Mountjoy had called in the shop, she had asked Mr Peach if his little boy could come to tea. All the time she smiled down and spoke pleasantly her eyes looked Sam up and down to see if he was really tidy enough to play with her Percy. Mr Peach, who was impressed by Mrs Mountjoy's fur coat and Jaguar car, said he was sure Sam would love to come. Sam got out of it by having a toothache: it was on account of that toothache he had to go to Mr Bason and have five fillings, but it was worth it, Sam thought. He had not been asked again, but Percy always smiled at him hopefully.

Now, when Sam glanced over his shoulder, he saw Percy was following him at a respectful distance. When Sam stopped, Percy stopped too. Sam walked more quickly and, Percy broke into a trot. At the bottom of the hill, the road bent round to the river and Sam could see Abe Tanner, sitting on the low stone wall of the bridge.

Sam knew Percy was just behind him. The thought that Abe Tanner might see them together and think he had invited Percy along, made his blood run cold. 'Get back home,' he whispered.

Percy looked at him with wide, blue eyes. 'I don't want you along of me,' Sam said, and walked on. Percy sidled up behind him as if playing Grandmother's Footsteps – when Sam turned again, he froze, still as stone. Sam became frantic, and swore.

Percy's eyes shone. 'Swear some more, Sam,' he implored softly. The surprise of hearing him actually speak, and the admiration in his voice, made Sam hesitate. Then he recognized that Percy was the sort of tittle-tattle who would be bound to repeat every forbidden word to his mother. 'Oh – go away and leave me alone, can't you?' he said.

Percy's eyes shone more brightly, this time with tears. It made Sam savage. 'Cry baby bunting, dadda's gone a-hunting,' he taunted, and Percy hung his head.

Sam darted towards the river. As he did so, two things happened. The local bus chugged into view on the other side of the bridge and a very gaunt, tall old lady in deep black appeared out of the Fisherman's Rest. The bus halted on the opposite side of the road and the driver glanced towards her, but she made no move. Instead, she lifted her head and whistled piercingly. At once, Abe Tanner, who had been hanging over the wall of the bridge and dropping sticks into the river, straightened up, hurried across the road, took her by the arm and led her over to the bus. Sam watched covertly while she climbed slowly aboard: he had heard about Abe Tanner's blind old granny, but he had never seen her so close before. She looked like a very old hawk in mourning, he thought, and then he wondered with a bump of his heart, whether the things people said about her were true.

The bus moved off. Sam walked slowly towards Abe Tanner who was standing on the bridge, watching him. Abe was a thin boy whose clothes were either too big or too small for him; today he wore faded cords that hung precariously on his hips and a man's old, collarless shirt. His hair was long and straight and hung over his eyes in a fringe like a sheepdog's. Through this fringe, his slanty green eyes looked brightly and dangerously at Sam.

'Whaddya staring at?' he demanded.

'I wasn't staring.'

'Yes you was. You was staring at me Gran.'

'I wasn't.'

'Anyone laughs at me Gran and I bash them up,' Abe Tanner said.

Sam knew this was not an idle boast. He changed the subject hastily. 'Shall we go up the quarry?'

'I said, anyone laughs at me Gran, I bash them up,' Abe Tanner repeated. He moved forward, fists clenched. Then he licked his lips and grinned. 'Peachey,' he said. 'Silly ole Peachey.'

The blood rushed to Sam's head. 'Shut up.'

'Silly ole Peachy.'

'Say that again.'

'Silly ole Peachey.'

'Say it *once* again and I'll bash your head off.'

Abe's eyes danced like chips of green grass. 'Peachey, Peachey, brown bread and gravy,' he chanted, laughing – or pretending to laugh – so much that he had to double over and hold his stomach.

'Oh, I'll scrag you,' Sam said passionately, not moving.

'You can't.'

'Can.'

'Can't. Yellow-belly.'

'Big-head.'

'Puff-ball. Peachey puff-ball.'

Sam let out a groan and dived forward, but Abe side-stepped and he caught only the flying hem of his shirt tail. Sam hung on to it. Though Abe was quicker, he was heavier and, once he had hold of him the battle was fairly joined; they tugged at each other's clothes, each other's hair, and then, this being too painful, got their arms round each other, grunting and groaning. Sam managed to get his legs wrapped round Abe in a scissor's grip but his muscles weren't strong enough to hold it for long and Abe was able to squirm round and butt him under the chin with the top of his head. Sam yelped and let go.

A horrified voice said, 'Why, Sam PEACH.'

Panting, both boys sat up. Mrs Mountjoy stood on the bridge, clutching her fur coat to her throat with one hand and Percy with the other. She looked at Abe indignantly. 'You dreadful bully, setting on someone smaller than yourself!'

'Sam started it,' Percy said.

'Well, I did in a sort of way,' Sam said uncomfortably.

Abe got up, thrust his hands in his pockets and leaned against the wall of the bridge, whistling.

Mrs Mountjoy inspected him. He had looked ragged and dirty before the fight, now he looked a proper ruffian. Beside Abe, Sam looked respectable enough for a party. Mrs Mountjoy said coldly, 'Whoever started it, I think you should go home now, Sam. I don't think your mother would like it if she knew the sort of boy you were playing with.'

Abe's green eyes shone. He looked steadily at Mrs Mountjoy and suddenly produced a most delicate, lady-like belch. 'Oh, beg pardon, I'm sure,' he said, and bowed most politely.

Mrs Mountjoy turned her back on him. Her face was red, but she smiled sweetly at Sam. 'Come along, dear,' she said. 'Percy and I will go with you a little way. Then you won't be bothered by this – this *person*, again.'

Sam gulped and swallowed. Suddenly, without his intending it and probably because he had been fighting so soon after his dinner, the most beautiful belch burst out of him, much louder than Abe's. So loud, it made him jump.

Mrs Mountjoy stared at him, her eyes shocked and disbelieving.

Sam was about to apologize when Percy said, 'Sam's been swearing too, Mummy.'

Mrs Mountjoy drew a deep breath. 'I can guess who taught him. Come along home, my darling.' She took Percy's hand and stalked away. Her back was stiff and straight as a poker.

While she was in sight, neither Sam nor Abe moved a muscle. Abe's expression was blank. When she disappeared into her house, Sam said, 'She's a beast, to pick on you like that.'

'Oh, it don't matter.' Abe gave Sam a shy grin. Sam grinned back. They both began to giggle and then to laugh. Helpless with laughter, they reeled across the pavement and clutched at the wall of the bridge.

When he had recovered, Abe said, 'I'm going home now.' He fidgeted a minute before adding, casually, 'Like to come?'

Sam's heart missed a beat. Though most boys in Castle Stoke would have liked to be friends with Abe Tanner, Abe made friends with no one: he kept his own company, as his grandmother did.

'Won't your Gran be at home?' Sam could not help asking.

'If the ole bus hasn't broke down.' Abe laughed, and then looked at Sam suspiciously. 'You scared of me Gran?'

Sam hesitated. Mrs Tanner was something of a mystery in Castle Stoke. In a town where everyone knew everyone else's business – sometimes before they knew it themselves – no one knew anything about Mrs Tanner, who her family was, or where she came from, only that she had lived for as long as anyone could remember in a shack on the site of the old mine workings on the Bent Hill, that she spoke to no one if she could help it, and came into town rarely, to collect her pension and drink a pint of rough cider at the Fisherman's Rest. But knowing little sometimes makes people gossip more. No one actually said Mrs Tanner was a witch, but they said she went out at night and walked the hills, alone. When lambs died in a cold snap or milk turned sour in the churn it was convenient to have someone to blame. A farmer whose favourite cow had fallen over the edge of the quarry, swore it was just after Mrs Tanner had passed by . . .

'Course I'm not scared of your Gran,' Sam said.

But he had hesitated too long. Abe's face was dark. 'Mebbe you'd best not come, then.'

'Oh please Abe, I do want to,' Sam begged humbly.

Abe kicked at a stone for a minute or two, dribbling it between his feet until it rolled into the gutter and down a drain. Then he said, 'Well – all right, then. So long as you don't mind goin' up through Gibbet Wood.'

CHAPTER TWO

A CHILL ran through Sam and settled on his stomach. He felt as if he had just swallowed a glass of ice-cold water. It was one thing to think about going to Gibbet Wood some day but quite another to decide, casually, on the spot, that this was where you *were* going – and this very afternoon.

'My Mum says I'm not to,' he said. The words came out before he could stop them.

'You scared of your Mam?'

'Course not. It's just that . . . well . . . just that . . .'

'You're just plain scared altogether,' Abe said in a quietly confident voice. He sounded pleased about it.

Sam looked at Abe wonderingly. Of course Abe was exceptionally brave and daring, but surely everyone was scared of Gibbet Wood?

'Scared yourself,' Sam said.

Abe laughed. 'Me? Scared?' He thrust his hands into the pockets of his sagging trousers and hitched them up with a contemptuous swagger. 'What's there to be scared of? I've bin there hundreds of times – thousands, just about.'

Sam whispered, 'Have you seen the Headless Hunter, then?'

'Who's scared of an ole ghost?'

'Me,' Sam would have answered if he had been honest. Instead he said, weakly, 'Well, I s'pose there's no chance in the daytime.'

The Hunter only rode at night, and only when the moon was hidden behind cloud. It was on one such night, long ago, that the Hunter had been riding home: the hunt had killed a long way off, near Caer Caradoc, and it was dark before he rode back, over the Bent Hill. He had been skirting Gibbet Wood when his horse was frightened by something – legend did not say what the something was, but perhaps even then Gibbet Wood was a place to fear – and his horse had bolted, running wild into the wood, under the low, sweeping branches, with the Hunter helpless on its back.

A low branch had snapped his head off, clean, like a sword. A farmer had found it, the long hair tangled in a tree, the eyes wide and staring. The body was never found, nor was the horse.

No one Sam knew had ever seen the Hunter's ghost, but plenty claimed to have heard his horse, thundering by.

Sam said, 'You c'n feel him, like a sort of cold wind. And the hooves come on and don't stop – they sort of ride *through* you.'

He shivered with pleasurable excitement. The Headless Hunter was not such a bad thing to think about, even to frighten yourself with, when the sun was hot and the sky was blue. In fact, if the ghost was the only scary thing about Gibbet Wood, Sam would have been there long ago. But besides the ghost, the wood contained a live, malevolent ogre. Farmer John who owned it, and the hill farm that went with it, was about seven feet tall; he had a long beard and one long fang like a sabre-toothed tiger; he ate his meat raw and anything – anyone – he caught in his wood he shot and hung on his gibbet for the crows to pick them clean. This gibbet, a spreading oak in the centre of the wood, was a terrible place. Older boys than Sam had been there and come back alive, but they spoke of it in lowered tones. The smell was dreadful, they said, but it was more than the smell, it was the general, unearthly horror of the place; the hanging skeletons, the bones, the skulls. Some of them were almost certainly human . . .

Mrs Peach told Sam not to listen to such tales. In the old days, she said, most farmers had a gibbet where they hung the vermin they trapped or shot – grey squirrels, foxes, carrion crows. The habit was dying: in this part of the country, Farmer John was the only one to retain it. It was nothing to be afraid of, and, as for eating his meat raw, as far as she knew Farmer John was a vegetarian.

Sam listened but did not believe her. Grown-ups knew nothing: they only thought they knew. And his mother had never been to Gibbet Wood.

He said hoarsely, 'If you're not scared, I'm not.'

Abe said patiently, 'I *tol'* you I'm not scared, didn't I?'

All the same, he seemed in no particular hurry to reach the outskirts of the wood. They had to climb the lower slopes of the Bent Hill, across the prickly stubble of the cut wheat and then a belt of pasture land. Here Abe seemed anxious to linger, picking blackberries. Sam liked blackberries, but this afternoon his stomach was fluttering and churning and the sight of Abe, picking great fistfuls and cramming them into his mouth, made him feel sick.

'Come on,' Abe urged him. 'They're good an' ripe.'

Sam shook his head. 'Mum'll be mad if I get stains on my shirt.'

'Aw – you great booby,' Abe said, but he looked at Sam's set face and added, more kindly, 'There's some smashin' cob nuts higher up, if you'd rather.'

They picked the cobs and crammed their pockets. Abe said, 'There's a better tree up the quarry. We c'd go there tomorrow, if you like.'

Sam sighed. The way he felt now, there might well not *be* a tomorrow. Who knew if they would even get out of Gibbet Wood alive? Then he remembered something. Something important. 'I can't, not tomorrow,' he said.

He had remembered what he had meant to say to his mother earlier that afternoon. His father had asked him to remind her and he had meant to, only it had been so difficult to get her to listen. 'Hey Mum,' he had meant to say, 'do you know what? *Rose is coming tomorrow*.'

Rose Prentice was his cousin who was coming to stay for six months while her parents went to America. Sam had not seen her for a long time because her father was a journalist and he and his wife and daughter lived a wandering existence, first in one European city and then in another. Rose was not going to America because she had been ill; her mother had written and said she needed country air and a quiet, settled life for a while. 'I can't say no, can I?' Mrs Peach had said. 'After all, she *is* my sister's child.' And she looked hopefully at Sam's father as if, after all, he might produce some reason why she *could* say 'no'. Mrs Peach was not unkind or inhospitable, but she was nervous of children, the way some women are nervous of strange, wild animals; she was afraid she might not understand a little girl well enough to look after her properly. But Mr Peach only smiled and told her not to worry, of course Rose must come, and of course it would work out all right. 'Sam will look after her,' he said bracingly. 'She'll be a nice friend for Sam.'

A nice friend for Sam! A chilly depression settled on Sam's spirits. He did not dislike girls, nor object to their company occasionally, but six months! It was more than a long time. It was an age, an eternity!

He let out a groan that made Abe look at him in surprise. Sam explained why he could not go to the quarry tomorrow. 'Dad and me, we've got to go into Shrewsbury to meet her. She's coming on the train from London. 'Course, I could come out after dinner, but I expect I'll have to stay home with *her*.'

The melancholy expression on Abe's face showed a proper appreciation of Sam's position. He cared for girls even less than Sam did. The girls at school avoided him because he was 'rough', meaning by this not that he tore their frocks and pulled their hair the way some boys did, but that he wore terrible old clothes and didn't speak properly. The girls did not admire Abe Tanner the way most boys did. Girls, Sam knew, thought a lot about love and marriage and were always fixing on one special boy to get engaged to, a proceeding which entailed a great deal of giggling and note-passing in class and writing on walls, no girl had ever tried to get engaged to Abe Tanner. The only girl who had ever shown an interest in him had been a farmer's pale, fat daughter in the second class who had wanted to reform him, and had enlisted her mother's support. Abe had been asked to tea; he had gone once, and that was enough.

'She said I had to wash a-fore I sat down,' he explained to Sam. 'Well, I went into the bathroom and I shut the door an' the next thing I knew was her Mam, bangin' on the door. She said she'd got a clean shirt for me that belonged to her boy an' he'd growed out of. An' d'you know' – there was horrified indignation on his face – 'she walked right in an' started scrubbin' away at the back of me neck. I thought it was a real liberty an' I tol' her so but she didn't tek no notice, she just went on scrubbin'. So I lets out a bawl you c'd hear in the next parish – she took her hands off like she'd bin stung, I c'n tell you. I never went agin – wasn't asked, neither,' he added with a grin. Then he shook his head gloomily. 'You'll have to watch out, Sam, a girl in the house'll hinder you properly.'

Sam found this cold comfort. 'I wish I'd remembered to remind my Mum, though,' he said guiltily. 'Dad said she'd probably want to do a few things, like getting in extra food and tidying up the spare room a bit. He said the covers on the bed were a bit grubby because Tarquin – that's one of our dogs – sleeps on it. Though I can't see she'd notice that, can you?'

'I don' know. Girls is different from boys,' Abe said.

This was indisputable. Sam's face grew long and glum.

Abe tried to cheer him up. 'I 'speck she won't stay long. Jus' for a little holiday, like.'

Sam shook his head. 'Six months. She's coming to school an' all.'

'Where's her Mum and Dad, then?'

'Gone to America.'

'America? That's a heck of a long way.' Abe looked thoughtful. 'Why don't they tek her, then? I reckon that's mean, leavin' her behind all that time. Don't they like her or something?'

Sam said no, he didn't think that was it. 'She's been sick, I expect they thought she'd get tired, with them rushing about all over the place.'

But Abe was not convinced. He said it looked to him as if Rose's parents had just got fed up and were getting rid of her and that, in his opinion, it was pretty mean. 'Parents are like that,' he said and looked, suddenly, so sour and stubborn that Sam did not argue further.

While they were talking they had walked slowly up the hill and were now almost at Gibbet Wood. They had been so absorbed in their discussion that they did not realize they had come so far until they felt a sudden chill: looking up, they saw they had come out of the sun and were standing in the lengthening shadow of the first trees. They stopped short. The wood looked very dark after the sunlit fields; dark and secret. A pigeon bubbled up in one of the trees and then fell silent. Everything was quiet and still. There was a smell of damp undergrowth.

Neither of them spoke for a minute. Then Abe gave a

little cough. 'P'raps you oughter go home and remind your Mam your cousin's coming. I mean, if your Dad *said* . . .'

'She'll have remembered by now,' Sam said. 'She knew there was something she'd forgotten. She'll worry at it till she does remember, she's always like that, my Mum.'

'But if your Mam doesn't want you to go in here, p'raps you oughtn't.' Sam's eyes were still dazzled from the sun and in the purple shade of the trees he could barely make out Abe's expression, but he thought he looked pale. 'I don't want to git you into trouble,' Abe said.

It was unlike Abe to be so thoughtful.

'My Mum's all right, *I* shan't get into trouble,' Sam said uneasily.

Abe frowned. 'You're younger than me. I gotta think of that.'

This stiffened Sam's pride. His limbs felt curiously clumsy and swollen, like stuffed bolsters, but it was now or never. He said, 'If we're going, we'd better get on. It'll be dark soon.'

It was dark enough as it was. The trees grew thick overhead and let in little light; only, here and there, a smoky shaft of sunlight like a taut, nylon veil. The wood smelt of autumn: their feet sank through the crisp top layer of this year's leaves to the spongy leaves of many past autumns. The ground was a tangle of briars and nettles that stung and scratched their bare legs. There were paths in the wood but they were overgrown; thorny branches whipped their faces and tore at their clothes. It was very quiet, so quiet that when something started up from a bush with a creaky, whirring sound, they both stopped, hearts thumping.

'S'all right. S'only an ole pheasant.' Abe whispered after a minute. The sound of his own voice gave him courage. He went on in a normal voice, 'D'you know what to do with pheasants? You git some brandy or some rum or something and you soak some raisins in it till they're good and soaked, then you leave 'em about an' the ole pheasant comes along and gits stuck into them an' goes on till he's drunk – blind drunk he gits, and he runs round in circles and falls down an' you pick him up and chop his head off . . .'

'Sssh,' Sam said, looking fearfully over his shoulder.

'S'all *right*,' Abe said cheerfully. 'There's no one about.'

Perhaps there wasn't. All the same, Sam could hear noises. Creaks, twigs snapping, soft, padding, rustling sounds. From being quiet and still, the whole wood now seemed to have come alive. As they pressed on again, Sam was dead afraid. The wood was bigger than he had imagined. And Abe, who had been here thousands of times, seemed just as lost as he was! Surely they had passed that tree stump before? And *that* tree, with the yellow fungus growing out of the trunk? Suppose they never got out, suppose they were lost for ever? First they'd get hungry, and then more hungry till hunger was a pain gnawing at their insides, and then they'd get too weak to walk any more and they'd just lie down and die. . . . They might not die in peace, either. There might be animals, real wild animals. His mother had said that there were still a few wild cats left in this part of the world. If she was right, what likelier place than Gibbet Wood? Though wild cats were a good bit smaller than tigers or pumas, they were quite as savage. More savage, in a way: you could never tame a wild cat and they had been known to attack human beings. If you were weak with hunger, they could jump on you and scratch your eyes out.

'Have you ever seen a wild cat, Abe?' Sam asked faintly.

Abe was standing still, his face lifted, his nose twitching.

'C'n you *smell*?' he said softly.

Sam thought he could detect a faint, putrid smell.

'Must be the ole gibbet,' Abe said.

Fear forgotten, they forced their way through a network of brambles and came to the edge of a small clearing

'Cor – look at that!' Sam said.

The smell was fearsome, but after the first shock he barely noticed it. The old tree, its long branches sweeping almost to the ground, was hung with corpses. Sam saw a grey squirrel, flat and transparent as a pressed skeleton leaf, thin as the finest tracing paper. 'It must've been there for years and years,' he said. Nervously, his eyes wandered further. But there was no sign of a human skeleton, only crows in varying stages of decomposition, more grey squirrels, rats, a hawk so far gone that he could only recognize it by the beak, a heavy, grey badger with a fatherly expression, and three foxes. Two of the foxes were skeletons, all vertebrae and grinning skulls, but one was more recent: a big, dog fox with its paws folded on its chest, jaws smiling slightly, looking neat and composed like a portly business man asleep after a heavy meal. 'He looks *alive*,' Sam whispered, in awe. 'He must be the biggest fox in the whole world.'

'He's dead, all right,' Abe said, and glanced slyly at Sam. 'Bet you daren't touch him.'

Sam swallowed. 'Who says?'

'I say.'

'Daren't yourself.'

Abe went forward at a run, slapped the fox in the belly, set it swinging and ran back to Sam without drawing breath.

Once set in motion, the body's weight jogged the branch up and down, giving the fox an even more horrible appearance of life.

Abe looked at Sam triumphantly. He said nothing. Sam set his teeth, shut his eyes and ran forward blindly. He touched the fox's brush and then, with sudden, desperate courage, swung it backwards and forwards like a pendulum,

27

lurching forward himself with the effort and saving himself from falling by clutching at the trunk of the tree. He opened his eyes. 'Cor – it's hollow. *Look*.'

There was a big hole, chest high, in the trunk. The boys peered in; light filtered from another hole, higher up, and disclosed a safe, smooth-sided hideaway. Sam said excitedly, 'I bet something's hidden there. I mean, it's a perfect place. If you got something to hide, I mean. Who'd come to look, when it smells so bad?' A marvellous thought struck him. 'Suppose Farmer John's got something he don't want any-one to see? He might have hung all these dead things here on purpose to keep people off . . .'

Fact was more in Abe's line than fantasy. Silently, he hoisted himself up to look through the hole, and reported that it was quite empty.

Sam was only momentarily disappointed. 'It u'd be a smashing place to hide things, though. You could hide there yourself if you were running from the police or something, or if you were a robber you could hide your loot – you could rob a train and just dash up here and put all the money in the tree and no one 'ud know. Or if there was a war on and you were a guerilla fighter, you could keep all your guns there.'

'There ain't a war on just at the moment, and there ain't no trains for miles,' Abe said coldly. 'An' you're shouting loud enough to frighten the crows . . .' He stopped and stood, tense suddenly and listening.

'What's the matter, Abe?'

'Hold your noise. Someone's coming . . .'

Sam strained his ears but heard nothing. Abe whispered, 'He's lyin' low – waitin' to git us.'

'Farmer John?'

Abe nodded. His eyes were bright; he had a wild, hunted look. 'We'll have to run for it. When I say . . .'

A twig cracked like a shot. *'Now ...'* Abe was off, leaping over a fallen stump. Sam could not move, his legs were stiff as iron. Abe stopped and doubled back like a hare, running past Sam. There was someone behind him. Sam had a nightmare glimpse of a giant with a great, red face, and then, miraculously, his limbs obeyed him and he was off after Abe, running faster than he had ever run in his life before. The tangly undergrowth that had been so difficult to push through on their way to the gibbet seemed nothing now: briars tore at his legs, his face, his clothes, but he did not notice them. All he was conscious of was that terrible voice behind them. 'Young vermin, just let me get my hands on you ... I'll learn you ... GET OUT OF MY WOOD.'

They were doing their best. But Sam was beginning to tire. His heart was pumping so, he felt it would burst in his chest. 'Abe, Abe,' he panted. 'I can't go any more ...'

Abe stopped for a second to let him catch up, but then he was off again. Red lights danced in front of Sam's eyes and a fresh fear seized him. Suppose – suppose they couldn't find their way out? The dreadful thought almost halted him, but he stumbled on for another minute, and then another. And luck was with them. They burst out of the wood not far from where they had entered it and pounded down the gentle, sunlight pasture to throw themselves under the cob nut tree.

They drew long, painful breaths. When his pulse had slowed, Sam murmured, 'Abe, what if he'd caught us?' and glanced back, shuddering, at the dark wood.

'Dono. I reckon he'd have shot us dead and hanged us up – like them other creatures.'

They said no more for a bit but just lay still on the cool grass while the sun sank low in the sky. Below them, the rooks began to wheel round their nests in the high trees on the edge of the football pitch.

Abe said, 'I best git home. Me Gran'll be wanting her tea.'

He stood up, stretched and yawned. 'Be seeing you,' he said and thumped Sam in the chest in a friendly fashion before he ran off.

Sam watched him a while, making his way round the hill along the edge of the wood, and then he walked homewards himself, whistling like a lark. The scratches on his legs and arms were beginning to hurt, he was stiff and sore and tired but he had a wonderful sense of well-being. He felt inches taller, a hero. He had been into Gibbet Wood and come out alive.

CHAPTER THREE

Rose Prentice said, 'A friend of mine had a poodle once but it wasn't allowed in the drawing room.'

She spoke reflectively, as if she were trying to get herself used to a house where large dogs occupied almost every chair, as well as the hearth before the fire. Lady, who was sharing the sofa with Rose – or, rather, taking up most of it – raised her head and thumped her tail inquiringly as if she knew she was under discussion. 'She won't bite, will she?' Rose asked nervously.

'Course not. Not Lady. Hero's the only one who's a bit nervy sometimes.' 'Nervy' was Sam's mother's word for bad-tempered. 'But she only bites men in uniform, like postmen,' Sam explained encouragingly. 'Don't you like dogs?'

'I don't know. We always lived in flats and hotels. Even if we'd had a house, I don't expect we'd have had a dog. My mother says they make things so dirty.'

Sam looked round the room. Was it dirty? It looked all right to him, but then dirt was not something he noticed much. There were a few patches of fresh mud on the carpet. He looked at his shoes: he had been up in the field with the dogs before dinner and had not bothered to wipe his feet. Mrs Peach never nagged him about that sort of thing – there would have been no point, Sam thought suddenly. The dogs brought in so much mud on their beautiful, silken paws, that his own contribution could only be a trifling matter.

He pointed this out to Rose. 'So it's really a sort of advantage, having dogs.'

'I don't get my shoes dirty,' Rose said.

Sam sighed. Rose looked as if she had never been dirty in her life. She was wearing a dress of pale pink wool, bought, so she had told Mrs Peach, in Paris, white socks and black patent shoes. In fact, her appearance was just as smart and citified as Percy Mountjoy's – only in Rose this was just bearable because she was a girl, and pretty. Sam thought her *very* pretty, though he would have died rather than say so. She had a pale skin, dark hair that curled softly at the ends and big eyes that were brown and shiny as conkers. Her arms and legs were slender and delicate. 'She looks as if she could do with a few square meals,' had been Mrs Peach's comment.

Since Rose's arrival, Mrs Peach had been bursting with good resolutions. She would take time off from walking the dogs and grooming them for show in order to bake cakes and pies to tempt Rose's appetite so that she could send her home, at the end of her visit, plump as a partridge. 'The child's got no colour,' she lamented to Mr Peach in the kitchen. 'It comes of living in stuffy old towns. Look how nice and brown Sam is!'

'Sam isn't so brown now,' Mr Peach said quietly. This was true: this morning, before going to meet Rose's train, he had taken Sam into the bathroom and removed a great deal of his tan with a face-cloth.

'Fresh air,' Mrs Peach said. 'She must have lots of fresh air,' and went at once to the living room, to send them out for a walk.

Sam's feelings were mixed. He did not object to being seen out for a walk with this pretty cousin. But what could they do, where could they go? Where could Rose go, in white socks and black, shiny shoes? Sam was too shy to suggest she might change her clothes. And suppose they met Abe? He knew how Abe felt about girls and Rose, surely,

32

was just the sort of girl Abe would most disapprove of. Though pretty, she was so clean and prim-looking.

But there was no sign of Abe. Sam had thought he might be waiting on the bridge, but he wasn't. There was only a group of boys busily engaged in launching a roughly made raft on the swift-flowing river. Two of the smallest boys crouched in the middle while the others pushed it clear of the bank. The raft began to leak at the seams as soon as it touched the water but it floated until some bigger boys climbed aboard, when it sank, spilling them all into the shallow water. Shouting and splashing, they made for the shore while the raft disintegrated and swirled away in the current.

Sam and Rose leaned over the stone wall and watched in silence. Sam knew these boys well, but since he was with a stranger they only acknowledged his presence with the briefest of nods and an occasional sly glance at Rose. A few of the oldest boys began to show off for her benefit, yelling, chasing each other and turning cart-wheels. After a while they tired of these antics and chased off across the football field.

Enviously, Sam watched them go. 'That was a rotten-awful raft,' he said. 'I made a smashing one last week. We made a sort of sail out of my shirt and we sailed right along, right down to the rapids. 'Course it's pretty dangerous there, I mean there are rocks and things, you got to be awfully careful.'

Rose was unimpressed. 'There couldn't be real rapids. It's a very little river.'

Sam sighed. He was beginning to feel hot and uncomfortably imprisoned in his best suit. But he was determined to go on being polite. 'What would you like to do?'

'I don't know. What is there to do?'

'I don't know.'

33

They walked slowly up the Town. 'Is this all there is?' Rose said. Sam did not answer: he felt too discouraged. They walked back down again, to the river.

'It's a very small town, isn't it?' Rose said. 'My mother says . . .' She hesitated and looked embarrassed.

'What?'

'She – she says Uncle – your father, I mean - used to be such an ambitious man. She says she can't understand how he can bear it, living in a little place like this.'

'Oh, Dad doesn't mind,' Sam thought a minute and decided that this was not quite true. 'He did say once he wanted to get a bigger shop somewhere, but Mum said – I mean there mightn't have been anywhere for the dogs.'

'My mother says she can't understand how anyone can be so da – so fond of dogs as Auntie is,' Rose said.

Sam knew she had been going to say 'daft about dogs,' and, in fact, he would not have been surprised if she had said something even less polite. He would not have minded. He was used to the idea that a great many people thought his mother extremely odd, and he did not mind that, either. She was his mother and he was used to her. He was going to say something of the sort to Rose, so that she would not feel badly about criticising Mrs Peach in front of him, when he saw Abe Tanner.

Abe Tanner was riding on a white horse.

It was a very old, white horse. A mare, so old that her spine had sunk into a deep, squared hollow in which Abe sat as comfortably as in an armchair. Horse and rider were approaching slowly across the bridge; as they drew level with Rose and Sam, Abe glanced slyly sideways. Then he looked away at once and fixed his gaze on the heavens.

'Abe . . .' Sam began doubtfully, but Abe tossed back his hair and clapped his feet against the horse's sides. The mare broke into a lumbering canter and then, as Abe beat his feet more frantically, into a wheezing gallop. They went up the Town with a clatter of loose stones. A few people, out in the street in their Sunday best, stopped to watch them go by. Halfway up the Town, the mare began to flag. Abe turned her and they descended slowly, the mare's hooves slipping on the steep incline. When they reached the football field, Abe set her at a gallop again. They went twice round the field. At the end of the second circuit, Abe reined the mare in, clambered on her bare back and stood triumphantly erect for a few moments while the old horse jogtrotted along. Then he dropped back into the hollow of her spine and set his heels to her sides.

'That's a friend of mine,' Sam said, torn between pride in Abe's prowess and the knowledge that he was showing off.

'When we were in London, my father took me riding in Rotten Row,' Rose said. 'Everyone looked at us.'

Abe cantered towards them, slowing the mare to a walk as he approached the bridge. He was having a hard time trying to pretend that he hadn't noticed them. Sam toyed with the idea of ignoring him, too, but he was too curious. When Abe was close enough, he asked, 'Where'd you get the horse, Abe?'

Abe looked up with a startled expression, as if he were wondering what queer stranger had spoken. 'Oh – it's *you*, Sam,' he said.

'Who'd you think it was, Farmer John?'

Abe smiled. 'Course I gotta horse.' He boasted unconvincingly. 'She's a thoroughbred. A real racehorse. Bin in the Grand National.'

The old mare's sides were heaving in and out like a pair of bellows.

'Bit past it now, isn't she?' Sam muttered.

'Oh, I dunno! She mayn't look much, but looks ain't

35

everything. She'll go like a young 'un when the fancy takes her. You'd be surprised. Once she gits going, you got to watch out. Gits the bit between her teeth – she's proper wild, really.'

Sam glowered disbelief for a moment and then capitulated. 'Can I have a ride, Abe?'

Abe reflected, then shook his head. 'She might set off with you.'

Her eyes did have a wild rolling look, Sam decided. And old she might be, but she was a big horse, heavy and powerful. Still, pride would have made him insist if Abe had not changed the subject. He patted a bundle of sacking he was carrying, fastened to his belt. 'D'you know what I've got here? Wanta see?'

Without waiting for an answer, he slid from the mare's back, looped the bridle over his arm and unrolled the bundle. Sam stared. 'Dead rat,' Abe said, unnecessarily.

It was a very large, dead rat. 'Where'd you get it?' Sam asked.

'Me Gran's fowl house. It was after the hens. I killed it with a stick. It was a terrible business,' Abe said.

Sam glanced at Rose. In his experience, girls did not care for dead animals. However impressed Rose had been by Abe's horsemanship, he would gain nothing by *this* piece of showing off. But to his surprise, Rose looked more animated than he had seen her up to now. Her face was pink, her eyes glowed. 'Why, it's simply *huge*,' she said. 'D'you mean you killed it all by yourself?'

Abe gave her a brief, casual look and nodded sternly. Then he turned his back on her and addressed Sam. 'It was got up in the corner. It's eyes were all red, like fire. I jus' whacked and whacked at it with my stick.'

Sam's heart burned with envy. He had never killed a rat.

'Course, a rat'll git you by the throat,' Abe said.

'I think it was terribly *brave*,' Rose burst out. 'I would have *died*.'

Abe fixed his gaze on a point two feet above her head. 'You jus' have to know how,' he said. He rolled up the corpse, tied the sacking with string and hitched it to his belt. He nodded at Sam. 'See you,' he said, and vaulted on to the mare's back.

Rose gazed after him as he trotted up the Town. Her lips were parted in admiration. Sam thought she looked stupid.

'We'd best get home,' he said. 'It's tea time.'

'You haven't got a watch so how do you know?' Rose asked.

'By my stomach,' Sam said in a surly voice. Not only did he feel hungry but also, for some mysterious reason, rather cross.

Rose glanced at him, opened her mouth and then shut it again. They walked up the hill without speaking.

Abe was waiting for them in a side alley just before the Peach house. His face was crimson. 'You c'n have it if you like,' he said in a strange, high voice and, leaning forward, dropped the bundle at Rose's feet. Then he dug his heels into the mare's sides and was off up the street as if the devil were after him.

'He must be plumb daft,' Sam said. 'What's he think you're going to do with *that*?'

Rose did not answer. She picked up the sacking bundle. Her eyes were alight and her cheeks red as apples.

'You look as if your walk's done you a power of good,' Mrs Peach said, when they burst into the kitchen. 'I was right, fresh air's what you need, my girl. You look a different child already.'

'Oh Auntie,' Rose cried, 'look what I've got. The most marvellous, dead rat . . .'

CHAPTER FOUR

'I THINK we can do some Vulgar Fractions this morning,'
Miss Pennyfather said. She spoke in a bright, cheerful voice
as if she expected her class to be delighted with this lovely
treat.

Although Sam was good at arithmetic, he groaned with
the others. Miss Pennyfather waited patiently until the noise
had subsided. 'Test Four. I want you to try really hard and
show me how much you have remembered from last term,'
she said, putting on an encouraging smile.

There were more groans. Miss Pennyfather stopped smiling. 'Anyone who has not finished will have to stay in during
the dinner hour.' She sat down behind her desk and began
to mark the compositions the class had written during the
first lesson, on 'How I Spent My Holidays.'

Comparative silence fell. When Miss Pennyfather said a
thing she meant it – her bite was every bit as bad as her bark
– so Sam applied himself to his arithmetic book. But the
harder he tried to concentrate, the more his ideas wandered.
To pass the time, he got a matchbox out of his pocket. It
contained a spider he had caught in the school lavatories
before prayers and brought into class with him as an insur-
ance against boredom. He released the spider and placed
him on the sloping top of his desk. The creature scuttled
this way and that. Sam tried to keep it within bounds by
barring its way with his pencil but it was an agile spider and
escaped quite soon, dropping neatly over the side of the desk
at the end of a long, thin thread. Sam twisted round to see

where it had got to, but it had disappeared. He ducked under his desk.

'Sam Peach.' Miss Pennyfather spoke without raising her head. 'If you have finished Test Four, you can begin Test Five.'

Sam looked at his arithmetic book. The mere sight of it made him yawn until the tears came. It was the sleepiest of sleepy days. The sun streamed through the glass and made the classroom almost unbearably hot. A faint smell of rotting vegetation rose from the water plants growing in jars on the window sill and mingled with the other educational smells of ink and chalk. The boy next to Sam was gazing out of the window where the top of the Bent Hill lifted its purplish sides through a shimmering heat haze. This boy appeared to have fallen into a kind of trance.

The boy on Sam's other side, across the aisle, was sucking pear drops and reading *Beano*. Beyond him, the cleverest girl in the class was beginning Test Five.

Sam wondered what had happened to his spider. He peered round. At the back of the class, Abe was chipping bits of a piece of chalk with his pen nib and mixing them into his ink well. He was completely absorbed in this task.

Sam yawned again, until his jaws cracked. His sleepy eyes fell on Rose who was sitting near the window. She was pale and worried. When she saw Sam looking at her, she lifted her arithmetic book and mouthed at him. 'I CAN'T . . .'

Sam was surprised to learn there was something Rose could not do. Before they left home that morning Mr Peach had asked her if she was nervous, going to this new school, but she had laughed and said, oh no, she was quite used to new schools as she had lived in four European capitals: Paris, Rome, Berlin and Vienna. She could speak French and German and Italian as fluently as she spoke English. Though Sam thought she was boasting, Mr Peach was impressed. 'You're a clever girl,' he said. To Sam's astonishment, Rose had not denied this. She had simply smiled prettily and said, 'Oh, I *like* school.'

Mr Peach had looked thoughtfully at Sam. 'I hope you'll set my son a good example, then. He could do with it. And I'm sure it will be nice for Miss Pennyfather to have *someone* in her class who wants to be decently educated.'

Sam was indignant. Though he found school intensely boring and had, himself, absolutely no desire to be educated at all, he thought it was unfair of his father to compare him unfavourably with Rose.

Now, looking at her troubled face, he could not help being pleased to see that she was not quite as clever as she seemed to think. But then his good nature asserted itself and he set himself to working out the answers to Test Four on a piece of rough paper. When he had finished, he folded the paper into a dart and looked up. Miss Pennyfather appeared to be busily occupied. Sam grinned at Rose and flicked the dart over to her desk.

Miss Pennyfather rose, walked across the classroom and removed the dart from Rose's fingers. She unfolded the paper and studied it.

Then she spoke. 'Who sent this?'

'Me,' Sam said, resigned.

'Not "me", Sam. *I*. I did.'

'Yes, Miss. I did.'

Rose said quickly, 'It's my fault, I asked him.'

Miss Pennyfather had thin eyebrows. She raised them and said, calmly, 'Well done, Sam. All your answers are correct. Now, since you found the Test so easy, you can turn to the last page and work out Test Twenty-Five.'

Behind Miss Pennyfather's back, the cleverest girl in the class looked at Sam and smirked.

'That will do, Sandra,' Miss Pennyfather said, without

turning round. She looked at Rose quite kindly. 'I believe you've not been to school in England before?'

Rose shook her head. Miss Pennyfather smiled. She had a thin, wrinkly face and she looked like a lizard when she smiled. 'Well, dear, you will have to learn that in English schools we try to do things for ourselves.'

'But I couldn't do the sums,' Rose said. She did not seem at all nervous of Miss Pennyfather, and this worried Sam. Miss Pennyfather was the worst teacher in the school. She was very strict and had a sly, sarcastic tongue. Sam tried to catch Rose's eye so that he could frown a warning at her, but she was looking up into Miss Pennyfather's face and did not notice him.

'You mean you've never done fractions before?' Miss Pennyfather asked.

'Oh, yes. I did them in my school in Paris and before that in my school at Vienna. But I was never any good at them. I've never been any good at all at arithmetic.' Rose spoke confidingly, as if she were talking to her best friend. 'My father says I just haven't got a mathematical mind, so it's a waste of time for me to worry about it. He says it's more important for me to concentrate on the things I'm good at, like languages.'

The classroom was deathly quiet.

'How many languages do you speak, Rose?' Miss Pennyfather asked mildly.

Rose told her. 'French, German and Italian. And my father says I'm to start learning modern Greek next year. He says I'm a natural linguist.'

She smiled proudly and happily at Miss Pennyfather. Sam almost groaned aloud.

Miss Pennyfather's tongue flicked along her lips. After what seemed to Sam a very long time indeed, she said, 'I am most grateful for your father's views on your education,

Rose. It is most unfortunate that I have to consider the rest of the class as well as you. I *do* hope you don't mind, if *just* occasionally we try to do a little arithmetic for their benefit?'

Rose turned first red and then so white that Sam thought she would faint. But Miss Pennyfather had not finished. She walked briskly back to her desk, faced the class, and said, 'Well, perhaps we had better not waste any more of Rose's precious time today. You may put your arithmetic books away, and I will give you back your compositions. You have all made a great many spelling mistakes. I want you to write out each mistake three times.'

She called out their names in turn. Sam got six out of ten for his composition and Neatness! Try Harder! at the bottom. Abe only got three out of ten but Miss Pennyfather looked encouragingly as she handed it to him and said, 'This is really *much* better, Abraham. I hope you are really going to put your *back* into your work this term.' She left Rose to the last. Rose went out to her desk, her feet dragging. Miss Pennyfather said, 'I'm afraid I could only give you two marks, Rose. You used so many foreign words that I could barely understand what you were trying to say.' She smiled her lizard's smile. 'Perhaps I should apologize for not understanding your composition, but then I am not as well-educated as you.'

About half the class tittered. The other half, which included Sam and Abe, sat stoney-faced.

'I'm s-sorry,' Rose stammered, so softly that Sam could barely hear her. 'B-but I've never written a composition in English before and all the other languages kept coming into my head.'

She looked wretched. Surely, Sam thought, even Miss Pennyfather must pity her.

She did, indeed, speak more gently. 'Well, I hope you

will try harder next time. If you are clever enough to speak four languages, you should be clever enough to write a simple composition in . . .'

A girl squealed loudly.

'*Now* what is it?' said Miss Pennyfather.

'A *spider*. . . .' Other girls began screaming and flapping their exercise books. Interested, Sam saw a spider – was it his spider? – run along the aisle to the front of the class.

'Be quiet at once,' snapped Miss Pennyfather. 'What a lot of nonsense! Haven't you seen a spider before?' The spider advanced towards her desk. Miss Pennyfather went red and sat down rather suddenly on her chair, drawing her feet up beneath it.

'Surely one of you can catch it?' she said crossly.

No one moved. The spider climbed up on to the dais.

Miss Pennyfather put on her most sarcastic voice. 'Surely all you big boys aren't afraid of spiders?'

Abe got up and came forward. He caught the spider and put it in a tin he brought out of his pocket.

'Thank you, Abraham,' Miss Pennyfather said. 'You really can be very helpful when you choose to be. Now, when you have all written out your spelling mistakes, we'll have Nature Study.'

Nature Study was Miss Pennyfather's favourite subject. She spoke about the beauties of autumn, the falling red and gold leaves, the bright berries in the hedgerows and the peacefulness of cut corn fields in the September sun.

Her class, being country children and therefore immune to the beauties of Nature, sighed and shuffled their feet.

'What else happens in autumn?' Miss Pennyfather said. 'It's not just the countryside that begins to go to sleep, is it?'

Hands shot up. 'Some animals do,' said the cleverest girl.

'Very good, Sandra. We call it hibernating, don't we?

43

Now, what animals hibernate, do you know? Yes, Abraham?'

To everyone's astonishment, Abe Tanner was on his feet. 'Squirrels don't for a start, Miss,' he said. 'People say they do but they don't. I mean I seed 'em, running 'bout the trees in the middle of winter.'

This was the longest speech Abe had ever made in the classroom. Miss Pennyfather beamed. Sam was puzzled by Abe's sudden interest in Nature Study and then, as Abe asked, and replied to, more and more questions, he grew suspicious. What was Abe up to?

It wasn't long before he was answered – at least partially. Before the school bell went at the end of the morning, Miss Pennyfather chose the Dinner Monitors for the term. She asked for volunteers and Abe's long arm shot up. Miss Pennyfather chose him first. 'Just to show how glad I am you are trying to be helpful and co-operative this term,' she said. 'I really do believe you are turning over a new leaf, Abraham. Keep it up and I shall be *very* pleased with you!'

Abe grinned awkwardly. Miss Pennyfather gathered her books and left the room. The class stampeded for the door.

In the playground, Sam saw Abe disappear into the lavatories. In his mind, suspicion grew into certainty. He was about to follow Abe when Rose said, 'Oh Sam, isn't she the most hateful, horrible *beast*? No one's ever been so horrible to me before.'

Sam thought it more important to advise than comfort her. 'You just shouldn't *tell* her things,' he explained. 'Not the way you did – about what your father says and all. That's the sort of thing always makes her wild. She hates to be told what your parents think. We found that out last year. It's beastly luck, having her two years running...'

Rose sniffed. 'She's stupid, then, as well as beastly and

horrible.' The colour came up into her face. 'And I don't see why Abe was making up to her as if he liked her. I thought that was mean, after the things she said to me!'

'I expect Abe's got his reasons,' Sam said.

The dinner bell went then, and they crowded into the school hall where the trestle tables were set up. The children fetched their dinners from a hatch at the side, but the Staff sat down at a table at the far end of the hall and waited for the Dinner Monitors to take their plates to them. Abe was a good deal taller than the other Monitors – who were mostly small, good, clever children – and Sam could see him easily, carrying first the vegetable dishes and then the individual plates, with slices of meat already cut, to the teachers' table. He saw Abe set a plate in front of Miss Pennyfather. She smiled up at him sweetly.

Then Abe fetched his own lunch from the hatch and sat down opposite Sam and Rose.

The Headmaster called out, 'Quiet, please.' No one was exactly quiet, but they talked instead of shouting. The headmaster said grace in a very loud voice and everyone began to eat.

Sam was on his third mouthful when a high scream came from the Staff table. The scream was followed by hysterical sobbing. Stunned silent, the whole school looked up to see Miss Pennyfather being tenderly escorted from the dining room by the Infant's teacher.

The headmaster was on his feet, red and scowling. 'Get on with your dinner,' he ordered, and sat down again.

Immediately, a torrent of shouting and giggling broke out. 'Silence,' the headmaster cried. The shouting quietened to whispers. No one got on with their dinner. At Sam's table, only Abe sat stolidly eating. Except Rose, who looked puzzled, all Miss Pennyfather's class had an expression of horrified glee on their faces.

Sam leaned across to Abe. 'Have you got another one? I mean, if you haven't, she'll *know*.'

'She'll know anyway,' Abe said. 'But I put another in the tin, just in case.'

'Another what?' asked Rose, innocently mystified.

'Spider, you eejit,' whispered the cleverest girl and suddenly spluttered with laughter. 'For what we're about to receive . . .'

'You mean Abe put it in her *dinner*?' Rose said. She looked at her own plate and shuddered. 'Oh, poor Miss Pennyfather,' she said.

Sam glanced at Abe and shrugged his shoulders. There was no accounting for girls.

CHAPTER FIVE

THE spider episode was the end of Abe's brief career as a model pupil. After the dinner hour, Miss Pennyfather returned to her form room red-eyed and grim-mouthed. She sent Abe to the Headmaster and set the class an extremely tricky spelling test. Abe returned, looking sheepish. He sat down at his desk, folded his stinging hands round the cold china of his inkwell and relapsed into his customary torpor for the rest of the afternoon. Miss Pennyfather ignored him. When the class was dismissed, she asked Rose to stay behind.

Sam and Abe waited for her in the playground. When she came out, she was tear-stained. 'She says I'm cocky. She says I've got to learn to be humble otherwise I'll never learn anything. I hate her like poison,' Rose said passionately. 'She went on and on till she made me cry.'

'Skinny cow,' Abe said, slowly and deliberately, so that Miss Pennyfather who had just appeared in the doorway, dressed to go home, could not pretend she had not heard him.

Her neck flushed up angrily. 'Abraham!' she said.

'Abe was just telling us about a cow his granny's bought,' Sam said. 'A rather thin cow.'

Miss Pennyfather glared at him. Sam returned her gaze innocently. Miss Pennyfather pursed her thin lips and said it was against the rules for pupils to hang around the playground after school. She would be lenient this time, but if she caught them there again she would have to give them a black mark.

They listened in silence. When she stalked off on her

long, heron-like legs, they followed at a safe distance. She walked with her head slightly on one side and one shoulder hunched up. Sam imitated her and Rose began to shake with silent giggles. Encouraged, Sam began to mimic her. 'If I catch you again, I'll have to give you a black mark. A *black mark*,' he repeated in a ludicrously high, wobbly voice, and Rose snorted hysterically, and put her hand over her mouth.

'Watch out,' Abe muttered, and Sam saw that Miss Pennyfather had stopped to speak to Mrs Mountjoy who had just emerged from her house, wearing her fur coat in spite of the exceptionally warm weather, and trailing Percy behind her. Mrs Mountjoy was looking coldly in their direction. She said something to Miss Pennyfather who began to talk energetically, waggling her head. Horror dawned on Mrs Mountjoy's face. 'She's telling about the spider,' Sam said out of the corner of his mouth. 'Just walk by and take no notice.'

The three children proceeded, expressions of vacant innocence on their faces. As they passed, they heard Mrs Mountjoy say, 'Well, Miss Pennyfather, *now* you see why I couldn't possibly allow my Percy to go to school locally! To think he would have to mix with a dreadful, common boy like that!'

Percy looked as if nothing would please him more. The look he gave Sam and Abe from behind his mother's back, was happy and admiring. He twisted round to watch them go, pulling the length of his tethered arm, and Mrs Mountjoy jerked him back without looking at him – just as if he were a little dog on a lead. 'Fancy having a mother like that!' Sam said.

Abe was glowering. 'Silly ole b . . .' he began. He glanced at Rose and amended what he was going to say. 'Silly ole cow.'

'She must be the most terrible snob to say that about common boys,' Rose said indignantly. 'My father says English people are just about the most terrible snobs in the world.'

Abe's eyes glinted green. He ducked his head shyly. 'If you like, you c'n have a ride on my horse sometime,' he said.

At tea, Rose and Sam fortified themselves with toast and dripping followed by drop scones. Cooking was not Mrs Peach's strong point and the scones were leathery, but the children ate a plateful with butter and cherry jam.

'Heavens above, what did you have for dinner?' Mrs Peach said when she saw the empty plate.

'Just squashed up spiders,' Sam said. 'They weren't very nice so we didn't eat much.'

'Oh, get along with you,' Mrs Peach said.

They got along. It was a long way to the old mine workings on the other side of the Bent Hill, though it would not have been so far if they could have taken the short cut through Gibbet Wood. Sam explained why they could not do this, curdling his own blood with accounts of the Headless Hunter and the terrible Farmer John.

'Course, Abe and I've been there lots of times. We went there Saturday as a matter of fact, but it wouldn't be safe for a girl.'

'I wouldn't be scared,' Rose said.

'You mightn't think you would now, but you'd be scared all right.' Sam dropped his voice to a hoarse whisper. 'The Headless Hunter rides through you like a cold wind, or he sits on his horse just a little way away, through the trees, and you think he's staring at you – it feels like he's staring at you – till you see he's got no head, only the stump of his neck with the blood all trickling down it.'

'Ghosts can't kill you,' Rose said.

'They can drive you stark mad, though. There's a boy over at Long Barrow who saw him one night and he went home with his face white and his eyes all staring and he's not spoken a word since. He's ever so old now but his Mum has to look after him and feed him just as if he was a baby.' Sam smiled, pleased with this anecdote which he had invented on the spur of the moment.

'How do you know he saw the Hunter, if he couldn't speak?' Rose asked.

'Oh. Well – he spoke *once*. When they found him – he ran home, you see, over the hill and he lost his shoes so that by the time he got back to his house his feet were all torn and bloody and he collapsed outside the door - *well*, when they found him, his mother picked him up and he cried out …' – Sam drew a long breath – '… he cried out, "Oh Mother, the Hunter, the Hunter …" and after that he was sort of struck *dumb* …'

Rose looked at him closely. 'I don't believe it,' she said. 'I don't believe in ghosts, anyway. My father says …'

But Sam was bored with Rose's father. He said quickly, 'Well, I can't take you, anyway. It's dangerous. My mother wouldn't want me to take you anywhere that's dangerous.'

'*My* mother wouldn't mind.'

'She would, then.'

'She wouldn't.'

'She *would*.'

'Wouldn't.'

'Would.'

Rose's eyes smouldered. 'I'll go with Abe, then. My mother wouldn't mind if I went with someone sensible, like Abe.'

Though Sam's heart swelled indignantly at this, he knew that the best thing to do with people who were deliberately baiting you was not to answer them. So he said nothing and walked ahead of Rose so fast that she had to run to keep up with him. By the time they were round the side of the hill, and out of sight of the town, they were both out of breath.

Here the pasture land ended. They scrambled through a hedge and came on to common land where there was nothing but heather and the low-growing purple fruits that are called blueberries or bilberries in some parts, but which Sam knew as wimberries. He crouched on his haunches and began to pick them, eating some, but secreting most of what he picked in his grubby handkerchief.

'What are they, Sam?' Rose asked in a small voice.

Sam kept silent for a minute longer, then he got to his feet and held out his handkerchief as a peace offering. 'You can have these if you like.'

'Thank you, Sam,' Rose said humbly.

'Don't mention it,' Sam was still rather on his dignity but he relaxed sufficiently to smile at Rose. She smiled back and they walked on, almost, but not quite, at ease with each other.

Higher up the hill, the wimberries thinned out and they walked on cropped, springy turf covered with dried sheep droppings. There was no sound except sheep baa-ing and a curlew calling overhead – *weee, weee*, with a lilt at the end of each note as if it were asking a question.

The top of the hill was a series of smooth, rounded bluffs. When they topped the second one, the mine workings came into view in a hollow that sloped gently away down the hill. Quite near them was one of the old shafts, very narrow and deep – so deep that when they threw a stone down it they counted to thirty-seven before they heard a splintery crack at the bottom. Rose asked what they had been mining for. Sam said it was something like basalt, though he didn't really know.

Further down the hollow were more shafts and several tumble-down looking shacks. Most of them had tumbled down in fact, but one still stood four-square, with smoke coming out of a tin chimney. Outside was a tethered nanny goat and a few hens, scratching. As Sam and Rose approached, Abe's Gran came out of the shack. The soft wind ruffled the white apron she wore over her black dress and feathered her thin, grey hair. Rose and Sam stood still and she stood still too, as if listening. 'She's blind,' Sam whispered, suddenly nervous, and the old woman turned her head slowly towards them. Then she whistled, shrilly.

'What's that for?' Rose moved close to Sam so that their arms were touching.

'Abe. She's calling Abe.'

They waited. Abe came, riding the white horse over the far bluff. He waved his arm and stopped to speak to his Gran. She went inside the shack and Abe got off his horse and led it towards them. His face was blank, like an empty window. 'She wants you to come down,' he said abruptly.

Slowly, they followed him to the shack. Rose slipped her hand into Sam's and he gave it an encouraging squeeze, though his own heart was thumping.

Abe's Gran was standing in the doorway. 'Good-evening,' she said. She was holding a tin mug in each hand.

'Good-evening, Mrs Tanner,' Sam said. Though he wasn't looking at Abe, he could feel Abe watching him. He went forward and took the two mugs. He gave one to Rose.

'It's goat's milk,' said Mrs Tanner.

Sam sipped at it. Rose did the same. It had a strong, cheesey taste but they barely noticed it. They were looking at Mrs Tanner.... The sun shone in her sightless eyes and on her old hawk's face, one side of which was oddly twisted and motionless. One side of her mouth smiled in the children's direction, the other drooped. She appeared to be watching them intently and Sam wondered uncomfortably if she was putting a spell on them. When she lifted her head his heart missed a beat, but she only said, 'Come here, Sam Peach.'

52

Sam put down his tin mug. 'Closer,' she said. He shut his eyes briefly and took one more step. She put up her two hands and moved them gently over his face: her fingers felt light and dry as dead leaves. Then she smiled with the one side of her mouth and said, 'Rose? I would like to meet you, too.'

Sam could feel Rose quivering as she stood beside him, but she lifted her face for the blind woman's touch and said, 'Thank you for the milk, Mrs Tanner.'

Sam glanced at Abe and saw he was smiling. Though he was hurt to realize that Abe had feared they might behave badly, he smiled back.

'Thank you, dear,' Mrs Tanner said, to Rose. One thin finger still trembled on the girl's cheek. 'Pretty child,' she said.

'Did you tell her Rose was pretty?' Sam asked, when Mrs Tanner had gone inside the shack and shut the door.

Abe shook his head. 'She just knows. She allus knows by touching people.' He paused, and went on in a low voice, 'She knows more'an that, too. She knows when people's bad – if I've bin and done something, it's not a bit of good my tellin' lies. She jus' knows when she touches my face ...'

Sam had a queer, hushed feeling, the sort of feeling he had had once or twice in church. Not when it was full, on Sundays, but on a weekday when there was no one else there. It wasn't a frightening feeling, but calm and peaceful. He didn't want to do anything, or speak – just to stand still and quiet in the sun.

Then Abe said, 'Well – ain't you going to have a ride of my horse?' and the spell – if it was a spell – was broken.

They mounted the mare in turn. She was as comfortable as she looked. Sam cantered her, and it was a gentle, lolloping motion like a rocking chair. Rose would not ride alone, so Abe led her up one side of the hollow and back again. Then they turned the horse loose and sat on the soft turf, in the dying sun.

'What's your horse's name?' Rose asked.

'Oh – jus' Whitey.'

'I'd call her something nicer. I'd call her Blanche. That's "white" in French.'

'She ain't a French horse, though,' Abe said.

Rose sighed. 'It's nice up here. It's a lovely view.'

The boys smiled. Town people always talked about lovely views. 'No one comes up here much,' Abe said.

Perhaps they were afraid of Mrs Tanner, Sam thought. But he said, 'I suppose there's nothing much to come *for*.'

Rose sat up, her hands clasping her knees. 'We don't want to bring anyone else up here, *ever*. We'll keep it quiet and empty like it is now. Just the three of us, that's enough.' She looked at the boys. 'We could be a gang,' she said eagerly. 'I've never been in a gang.'

'I've been in thousands, just about,' Sam said, feeling superior. 'You get bored with gangs, after a bit.'

Rose wasn't put off. 'We'd never get bored with *this* one. We could call it the Bent Hill Gang.'

There was an unimpressed silence.

'Or the Peach Gang,' Sam said.

Abe shook his head. 'I don't like that.'

They racked their brains. Rose looked at the old mare, peacefully cropping the grass. 'We've got a white horse,' she said. 'We could call it the White Horse Gang.'

'That's not bad,' Sam said in a grudging voice. 'Course, a white horse is lucky. I mean it's lucky if you spit when you see one and touch your shoe.'

Abe lay on his back and chanted, 'White horse, white horse, give me good luck, today or tomorrow, I'll pick something up.' Then he sat up and looked shyly at Rose. 'It 'ud be like calling it the Lucky Gang, wouldn't it?'

They both looked at Sam. 'All right,' he said. 'We'll call it the White Horse Gang. And we got to have a secret sign.'

Giggling, Rose placed her left forefinger against the side of her nose. Sam suggested that they should use the other hand at the same time, and pull at the lobe of the right ear, but Abe said they didn't want to make it too obvious.

'And we'll sign our names backwards,' Rose said. She looked blissfully happy, so happy that neither boy could bring himself to protest that this was a childish device. They practised with a pencil stub on an old bus ticket Sam had in his pocket. Esor and Mas and Eba. 'That's lovely,' Rose sighed. 'Course, we ought really to sign in *blood*.'

'Blood's for kids,' Sam said. He had once got a septic finger from pricking and extracting blood for this purpose. 'What we want more is a *reason*. A gang's got to be *for* something – like stealing, or being a guerilla fighter when there's a war on, or robbing the rich to give to the poor like Robin Hood ...'

'Enemies,' Abe said suddenly. 'What we got to have is enemies. Then there's some sense in having a gang.'

'*I* know,' Sam said. 'We fix on our enemies and we get a plank and we make notches in it each time we do something to them ...'

'Like *killing* them?' Rose breathed. Her eyes sparkled.

Abe shook his head. 'Killin's a bit silly. I mean it's better if it's something we *can* do ...'

'Like putting a spider in Miss Pennyfather's dinner,' Sam explained. 'Best thing 'ud be if we each choose our special enemy. That'll be three altogether, so we got to get three planks.'

'Miss Pennyfather's mine,' Rose said.

Abe walked over to one of the deserted shacks and wrenched off a piece of wood.

'Cut a notch in it,' Rose cried, hugging her knees with excitement.

'In a minute.' Abe pulled two more planks away. 'Mrs Mountjoy for me,' he said, and, sitting down, began to carve away at Miss Pennyfather's plank with his clasp knife.

Rose looked at Sam. He tried to think. He had no real, personal enemy, no one who had been rude to him, like Mrs Mountjoy, or unkind, like Miss Pennyfather. 'Farmer John,' he said.

Abe frowned. 'What's he done to you?'

'What d'you mean, what's he done to me?' Sam said truculently. 'He chased us out of his wood, didn't he?'

'Well – mebbe.' Abe looked doubtful. 'It's his wood, ain't it? And we might've bin poachers or something.'

'We weren't though, were we? And anyway, you said he'd have killed us if he'd caught us and strung us up . . .'

'I know I *said*. But . . .'

'Farmer John is my enemy,' Sam said firmly. 'I can choose, can't I?'

Abe said no more. He was silent for a while, but as he was often silent, Sam paid no attention. They decided to stand the pieces of planking upright in the earth, like three tombstones. This was more difficult than they had expected as the cropped turf was tough to cut and the earth beneath close-packed and solid. By the time they had finished, their backs and arms were aching, the orange sun was blinking low over Gibbet Wood, and it had grown much colder.

'Auntie'll be worried,' Rose said. 'It'll be dark going home through the fields.'

'P'raps we'll see the Headless Hunter,' Sam said slyly. 'But you won't mind that, will you? You don't believe in ghosts.'

Rose shivered, looking pinched.

'You'd best go home by the road,' Abe said. 'I'll see you a piece of the way.'

It was dusk by the time they reached the road, and Rose

56

was flagging. Luckily, Mr Jones, who kept the Castle Bakery, stopped almost at once to give them a lift in his van. Before they climbed in the back, they said good-bye to Abe. Rose laid her forefinger against the side of her nose and said, softly, so that Mr Jones would not hear, 'Good-bye, Eba.'

'Good-bye Esor. Good-bye Mas.'

'How's your grandma, boy?' Mr Jones called, above the noise of the engine.

Abe did not answer. He faded like a shadow into the paler shadow of the hedge.

When the van had started up, Mr Jones repeated his question, 'How's Jess Tanner these days? Still busy with her broomstick?'

Sam pretended not to hear him.

Mr Jones laughed. 'Funny company you keep,' he remarked, and grated into bottom gear as he climbed the side of the hill.

CHAPTER SIX

'FARMER JOHN doesn't look the way you said.'

'How d'you know?'

'Auntie pointed him out at the market this morning,' Rose said.

'Oh *Mum*.' Sam spoke with airy contempt. '*Mum* wouldn't know. I expect it was someone quite different. Dad says my Mum wouldn't know her own mother if she met her in the street.' Since Sam's – and Rose's – grandmother had been dead for fourteen years, this was hardly something that could be put to the test.

'He looked quite ordinary,' Rose said. 'Short and fat.'

Sam sighed. 'Then it couldn't 've been him. He's the tallest man you ever saw, almost a giant, really. I *told* you Mum wouldn't know.' A thought struck him. 'Still, I suppose he'd be gone to market somewhere, seeing as it's Friday.' It was the third Friday in the month and they had a holiday from school because a girl in the top form had won a scholarship to the grammar school in Shrewsbury. 'Tell you what,' Sam said, inspired by the thought of Farmer John's likely absence, 'we could go into Gibbet Wood.'

This did not produce the effect he had hoped for. 'I've been already,' Rose said.

Sam stopped still. 'You *never*.... When?'

Rose smiled. 'Abe took me. Last week, when you were in bed with your head.' (Sam had knocked himself out falling out of a tree and been put to bed for a day for fear of concussion.) 'Abe said not to tell you unless you asked,' Rose went on. She looked pleased at Sam's astonishment – and

58

rather smug, Sam thought. 'I wasn't scared a bit. Abe said there was no need because Farmer John's all right, really.'

'Oh – he just *said* that. He's scared himself, all right. I expect he just said that because you're a girl.'

Rose went pink. 'He did *not*. Abe says Farmer John can't be so bad because he owns the land where the mine is and he lets his Gran live there rent free.'

'What for?'

'I don't know. Perhaps just because he knows she's poor.'

Sam shook his head. 'Farmers aren't like that,' he said with conviction. 'Specially not Farmer John. Why, he's the *meanest* man, everyone knows that.' He thought for a minute and then the reason for Farmer John's apparent generosity came to him. 'Perhaps he has to let her live there, have you thought of that?' he asked excitedly. Rose looked puzzled. 'He's scared of her,' Sam explained. 'Scared she'll put a spell on him. She does, you know. Don't you remember what it was like, that time we saw her? When she touched our faces ...' He gave a shudder. 'I could feel something – something sort of tingling through me.'

'I didn't feel anything.'

'Perhaps she didn't try to put a spell on *you*. I think she did on me. I felt real queer for a minute, as if I couldn't move.'

'You're just making it up. You're always making things up.'

'I'm not.' Sam was honestly surprised at this criticism. Though they had met Abe at the shack several times since that first evening, Mrs Tanner had not been in evidence and Sam's imagination had been free to work. He was now quite convinced that he had, indeed, felt very strange when she had touched his face. 'I'm not making it up,' he said indignantly. 'Why, everyone knows about her, there's all sorts of stories. ...' He sought one that would impress

Rose. Broomsticks and cats were too ordinary. 'She hasn't got a shadow,' he said in a hushed voice, 'that's one way you can always tell. And she's always cold. Don't you remember how cold her hands felt? And even if she doesn't touch you, just stands near, you can feel the cold coming from her like a sort of mist. . . .' He shivered, as if he felt a sudden, icy wind.

'Her hands *did* feel cold,' Rose said uncertainly. She looked at Sam for a minute. Then the colour came up into her face and she stuck her nose in the air. 'I think it's plain mean, talking about Abe's Granny like that!'

Sam felt faintly ashamed. He changed the subject. 'Weren't you really scared in Gibbet Wood? Not even a little bit?'

Rose hesitated. 'Well – it's a horrible smell, up by the gibbet. And I thought it was beastly, killing the badger. But Abe says badgers go after hens and young pheasants just like foxes. Abe says Farmer John lets the shooting in the wood and he hangs all those creatures up on the gibbet just to show he's keeping the vermin down.'

'He's a dead shot,' Sam said. 'Mr Jones, that's the baker, says he remembers when he went harvesting up at Farmer John's once, and Farmer John used to ride his horse round the field and shoot the rabbits and foxes as they came out of the corn – galloping full tilt all the time. Mr Jones says if he missed once he reckoned he was wasting ammunition, but *he* never saw him miss. He says Farmer John 'ud drop the fox dead even if all he could see was just a wavy line in the corn. Farmer John's just about the deadest shot in the county. And he isn't partic'lar what he shoots at, neither. I reckon you was lucky, going into Gibbet Wood like that. If he'd seen you, he'd have shot you dead and hung you up on the gibbet for the crows to peck at.'

'Don't be silly.'

'*Abe* says so,' Sam said cunningly.

Rose looked doubtful. 'You can't go round shooting people, though, it's against the law.'

'Farmer John don't worry about the *law*. He shot a poacher in the bottom last year and there was a case about it, but Farmer John got off. The man was trespassing, see? Loitering with intent. And that's what you were doing, just about. Abe shouldn't have taken you into Gibbet Wood, he knows it's dangerous,' Sam said virtuously, and added a phrase grown-ups often used. 'I don't know what he was thinking about, I really don't.'

He shook his head with a little sigh and glanced sideways at Rose to see what effect he was having. He saw she was looking subdued now, and felt somewhat mollified. He had really been very hurt and angry. Not only because Rose and Abe had been into Gibbet Wood without telling him, but also because it appeared that they were conspiring together to make Farmer John appear a less worth while enemy than their's.

Sam was very conscious that he had not yet marked a notch on Farmer John's plank. In fact, none of them had attempted to score him off at all! There were no notches in Mrs Mountjoy's plank, either, but at least they had tried: Sam had been in dire trouble with his father for mimicking her behind her back one day when she came into the shop. But mimicking and cheeking, they had decided, were not enough. Nor was the dead rat – not Abe's dead rat, but one Tarquin had killed in the field and Rose had placed in Miss Pennyfather's desk – since it had not, apparently, distressed Miss Pennyfather at all. She had merely used it as an excuse to give them an extremely long Nature Study lesson on the habits of the rat, including a graphic description of various rat-borne diseases like bubonic plague which put Rose – and most of the girls in the class – off their dinner.

The only notch so far had been marked up by Abe.

This irritating thought lingered at the back of Sam's mind long after they got to the quarry and found it full of shrieking boys. The quarry was forbidden by most parents because of the dangers of falling rock: as a result all the boys in Castle Grove went there whenever they got the chance.

This afternoon, one boy had acquired an old barrel and was charging threepence for the pleasure of rolling down inside it. Sam and Rose had no money. 'I can owe you,' Sam offered, but the boy shook his head. Since it took a long time to get the barrel back up again after each descent, there were plenty of boys waiting with ready cash in their pockets.

'Meanie,' Sam said, disconsolately kicking a loose stone. He was always short of money. It seemed to him that his parents were remarkably stingy compared to the parents of other boys. 'I only get ninepence,' he grumbled. 'What's *ninepence*? Jim Leek gets half a crown – *and* a shilling from his Granny!'

He tried to cheer himself up with the thought that he would be very much richer in a couple of months' time. For several years past, he had helped his father plant part of their top field with fir trees for the Christmas market in return for a small share of the profits.

'I should get a couple of pounds, I should think,' he told Rose proudly. Then he sighed. Christmas was a long way off. 'I wish I could dig some up now,' he muttered.

'Who'd want Christmas trees in September?' Rose asked.

Sam did not answer. An idea – a most marvellous idea – had suddenly come into his head. His cheeks went red. 'Hey Rose,' he said, 'd'you know what?'

But Rose wasn't looking at him. 'Where's Abe?' she said, looking round the quarry. Sam decided that his idea could wait until he had her whole attention and joined in the search.

They found Abe some way away from the top of the quarry, lying on his stomach and chewing grass.

'Thought you was never coming,' he complained.

'We looked in the quarry.'

'All those silly kids, playin' kid's games,' Abe said scornfully.

'What'll *we* do then?' Sam asked.

'Dono.' Abe spat out the chewed grass and got up lazily, yawning and stretching.

They wandered away from the quarry and picked a few wimberries but they were wrinkled and over-ripe. Climbing to the top of the highest bluff, they lay idly on the turf and looked down at the valley where an evening mist was beginning to spiral up over Gibbet Wood.

Sam sat a little apart, hands locked round his knees. The others sighed and yawned. Then they looked at Sam and thought he did not seem as bored as they were. He stood up suddenly and began to pace backwards and forwards, his face intent. From time to time his lips moved silently.

'What you doing, Sam?' Rose asked curiously.

'Thinking . . .'

'That's a change. I thought you looked a bit tired,' Rose said.

Abe laughed, but Sam was not offended. He whirled round to face them. 'Just listen a minute,' he said. 'I've got a fabulous idea. You know Miss Pennyfather?'

They nodded. 'Well you know what she's like, always on about Nature and how wonderful it is the way things grow and that?'

They nodded again.

'Well, you know those Christmas trees . . .'

Squatting on his haunches, he told them his plan.

'I've a present for you, Miss Pennyfather.'

'Have you, Sam. That's – er – that's very kind.'

Miss Pennyfather was unaccustomed to receiving presents from her form. She smiled rather stiffly as Sam placed a small Christmas tree on her desk. 'I just thought you might like it,' Sam said. 'I know you like to watch things growing. I mean, you're always telling us in Nature Study. If you like I could plant it for you in your garden.'

Miss Pennyfather eyed him suspiciously: it was her impression that Sam was usually asleep during her Nature Study lessons. But the expression on his freckled face was so shyly innocent that Miss Pennyfather felt ashamed of herself for doubting his kind intention.

'Why, this is most thoughtful of you, Sam. It's a lovely present and if you plant it for me it will give me even more pleasure. I shall enjoy watching it grow . . .'

She looked quite different when she smiled like that, Sam thought. So different that he began to feel slightly ashamed too. He might, even, have changed his mind about going through with the plan if she had not reverted to her normal manner and said, 'I should be even more pleased, Sam, if I could see your interest in your school work growing too! If I could see your mind putting down roots and stretching out its branches just like this little tree! Your mind is a growing thing like everything else in Nature, Sam, have you thought of it like that? But it needs effort to help it as a tree needs good soil and water . . .'

She went on to liken Sam's mind not only to a tree but also to a flower, opening from its tightly curled bud. Sam shuffled his feet and hated her.

The tree had been planted in Miss Pennyfather's back garden. She inspected his handiwork. 'You've made a good job of it, Sam. You see, you really can do things well, when you try.'

'It looks a bit small,' Sam said, 'but I expect it'll grow a lot bigger quite soon.'

'Oh, I shan't be impatient, dear,' Miss Pennyfather said. 'Growing is like learning, a slow and steady business. But slow and steady wins the race, doesn't it?'

'Yes Miss Pennyfather,' Sam said.

Sam and Rose went to bed early, feigning tiredness after tea. Mrs Peach, who had an unsuspicious nature, believed them.

'Both fast asleep,' she told her husband when she had peeped into their darkened rooms before taking the dogs for their nightly walk.

Of course, they were not asleep. Fully dressed except for their shoes, they lay stiffly in their beds until they heard Mrs Peach calling the dogs. 'Tarquin, Lady, Lancelot, Hero. . . .' The front door banged.

Almost immediately, the boom of loud voices, accompanied by shots and cries, came from the television set. Mr Peach was a little deaf, but disliked admitting it, even to his wife: he always waited until he was alone before turning up the sound. Sam knew that his father would not hear them if they thundered down the stairs in hob-nailed boots, but, to make doubly sure, they crept to the back door in stockinged feet.

It was a dark night. The moon was full, but a thick mist had blanked out the sky. It was thick in the garden, too, striking chill through their clothes and settling in glistening drops on their hair and lashes.

'It's cold,' Rose moaned.

'Ssh,' Sam warned her. He disappeared into the garden shed and emerged with something in his arms, staggering under its weight. 'Why, it's almost as big as me,' Rose whispered, and stifled a giggle.

'We got to be quick,' Sam panted. 'Take the spade.'

Clutching their burdens, they made their way to the end of the garden and into the field. Miss Pennyfather's garden was some way along, abutting on to the Peach property. As they approached her back fence, Sam stood still, his arms aching. 'Eba,' he called softly.

The answer came. 'Mas, Esor ... and Abe appeared, a dark shape between the twisting pillars of mist. 'I made a hole in the fence like you said, Sam.' He peered at what Sam was carrying and laughed silently. 'Don't know as it'll be a big enough hole, though.'

But it was. A few minutes' struggle, and they were standing in Miss Pennyfather's neat, narrow garden among some gooseberry bushes. They made their way slowly and stealthily towards the house and then stopped still, their hearts sinking. From Miss Pennyfather's kitchen window, a light suddenly shone out, diffused and yellowed by the mist, but still showing up the little tree Sam had planted, and the silvery lawn for several yards around it.

Sam plumped down his burden despondently. 'We can't do it, she'll see us.'

'Jus' wait a bit,' Abe said.

They waited. They could see Miss Pennyfather's head bobbing over the sink as she washed her supper dishes. An owl hooted once, a long way off, and then there was silence except for the sound of their breathing and a tiny rustling of leaves. A wind had got up and swirled the mist into strange shapes. Rose shivered, not from the cold. 'Let's go home,' she whispered.

'Ssh ...'

'We'll get our death if we stay here.'

'Jus' another minute,' Abe said.

The light snapped out and the garden seemed very dark. 'We shan't be able to see,' Rose said, a catch in her voice.

'Shut your eyes a minute. They'll get used to it,' Abe said.

He seemed to see better than they did. He led them forward to the small tree. 'Did you dig the hole good and big, Sam?'

'Big as I could. She was watching.' Sam stifled a laugh. 'She said, that's a big hole, and I said you got to make the hole big to give the roots room to grow . . .'

The soil was still loose round the fir tree. One quick pull, and it came up. Rose held it and Abe set to work to enlarge the hole with the spade. 'That'll do. Now Sam – quick!'

Sam had unwrapped the sacking from round the roots of the new tree. He lowered it carefully into the hole, sprinkling loose soil round the roots and then pressing it down firmly, the way his father had taught him.

'Hurry,' Abe breathed.

'You got to do it *properly*,' Sam told him. 'Otherwise it won't look right. It's got to look as if it had *grown*, overnight.'

Rose gasped as an upstairs light snapped on. They stood for a moment as if turned to stone, but no one came to the window.

The light showed them their handiwork: the new tree, standing a good three feet taller than the old.

They only dared admire it for a minute. When Miss Pennyfather came to draw her bedroom curtains, they were gone. She did not notice the tree, but it would be the first thing her eyes lit on, in the morning.

'She's going to get a fearsome shock,' Abe said, when they were safe in the field again.

'Nature is *wonderful*, children.' Sam mimicked Miss Pennyfather's high, reedy voice. 'Why, the tree Sam Peach gave me, grew a good three feet in one night!'

Rose giggled nervously. 'What'll she do, Sam?'

'She can't do nothing,' Abe said. 'She'll jus' have to keep it to herself. She'll feel a right ole eejit, though.' He grinned happily. 'It was a great ole idea, Sam.'

Sam almost burst with pride. 'We oughter to do it *again*,' he said, inspired. 'Get a bigger tree tomorrow night an' the next night an' . . .'

Abe shook his head. ''Twouldn't do. Even if we could – an' it 'ud be much harder with a bigger tree - jus' once is enough. If you do it again, she'd *know*. This way she'll never be quite sure – she'll wonder and wonder and she won't dare tell anyone, case they thinks she's daft.'

This was a more subtle approach than Sam had thought of. 'Why – she'll go raving *mad*,' he said with satisfaction. 'I reckon it's worth a good deep notch on her plank, don't you, Eba?'

Abe nodded gravely. 'I reckon so, Mas,' he said.

They walked back towards the Peach garden. Abe said good-bye and vanished into the mist. Rose looked after him. 'Poor Abe, going back all that way on his own,' she said. 'Past Gibbet Wood.'

Sam thought that Rose would never worry like that about him, if he were going home alone. He said, rather crossly, 'Oh, Abe's never scared. You said so.'

CHAPTER SEVEN

CERTAINLY, Abe was not scared as Sam or Rose would have been. He was used to loneliness and was as much at home in the fields and woods after dark as a badger or a fox. Ordinarily, the night held no terrors for him.

But tonight was not ordinary. Once the mist had closed about him, he began to feel not frightened, exactly, but uncomfortable. The mist dampened all the sounds – cows champing, trees creaking, the rustling of small animals in the hedgerows – that would normally have made the country night familiar. All he could hear was the sound of his own footsteps, squeaking on the wet grass. When he stood still and listened, there was nothing else: he was alone in a silent, white world.

It was the silence that began to make him afraid. He dared not even whistle to keep his courage up.

Something loomed out of the mist and he broke into a cold sweat – colder than the chilling mist about him. But it was only a cow that lifted her head and gazed at him with brown, mournful eyes. His relief was heartfelt. 'Oy, oy,' he shouted and clapped her on her bony rump, but when she lumbered off into the mist, he was alone again.

He began to fear he might lose his way. He knew every field, every tree and rocky outcrop on the Bent Hill, but things seemed to change in the mist, become strangely shaped or insubstantial. Here was the cob-nut tree – but was it *the* cob-nut tree? Hands were a better guide than eyes tonight. He closed his eyes and felt the trunk, sliding his hand up to the familiar fork just above his head. Yes, it was the tree, all right: a little further, and he would come to the edge of the wood. Once there, all he had to do was to skirt it, keeping it always on his right hand side.

All the same, he was reluctant to leave the tree. It seemed friendly and solid. He lingered, but the increasing chill, seeping through his tattered clothes, drove him onwards in the end.

Higher up, it grew windier. The mist distorted the sound of the wind in the trees and turned it into a booming noise, a foghorn sound, hollow and lonely. The mist became thinner in some places and thicker in others. There was no constancy about it: it would suddenly lift as if some unseen hand had raised a curtain, revealing a bush ten yards away, every twig distinct and glistening, and then, before Abe reached it, the mist would descend again.

He pushed on doggedly. Now he was at the edge of the wood: briars lifted from the ground and caught at his legs, unseen branches twanged against his face and showered him with water drops. He set his teeth and stumbled down hill a little, away from the wood. The wind seemed to have dropped and there was now no sound at all.

No sound – and *then* he heard it: a drumming noise, so faint at first, that only sharp ears could catch it. Abe heard it and stood still. It was the thudding of hooves on turf. His breath stabbed sharply in his throat as he stood, cold and listening. He couldn't make out where it was coming from, ahead of him or behind? And then, suddenly, it seemed to be all around him, a terrible, drumming sound that made his heart stand still and the sweat break out on his forehead again. 'The *Hunter*,' he breathed. He remembered all Sam had told him – all that he had dismissed as kid's talk, just kid's talk. Now he feared it was true. Why, he felt so cold, it was as if he had turned to ice.

The hooves came closer and closer. The sound seemed to

fill the world. He gave a little, choked moan and put his hands over his eyes. 'Don't let me see him,' he prayed inwardly. 'Just don't let me *see* him . . .'

Something bumped him between the shoulder blades and almost threw him down. With a wild cry he turned, arms flung wide . . .

It was the white horse. As he stared at her, joyously, unbelievingly, she bumped him again, gently, in the chest.

'Whitey,' he whispered. 'Oh, Whitey . . .'

It was like a miracle. 'Oh Whitey, you must have known,' he marvelled, wrapping his cold arms about her and burrowing his face into her warmly steaming neck. 'You shouldn't be here, y'old fool. Not in someone else's field. I'll have to tether you up, that's what I'll have to do, or we'll be in a whole heap of precious trouble . . .'

He scolded her lovingly and she blew through her nose and lowered her head to crop the grass which was so much richer and greener than her legitimate pasture.

Abe tugged at her mane and called her gentle names, all the endearments he had never used to any other living creature. She was his own, his beauty, his good old mare, the only thing he loved or could remember loving since his Gran had bought her three years ago from the blacksmith at Long Broughton, who had said she was fit for nothing now, but the knacker's yard. 'There my lovely,' Abe murmured as he scrambled on to her back and twined his hands in her long, coarse mane. He dug his heels into her ribs. 'Git on now,' he said.

They jogged comfortably along. She had no bridle and Abe could not guide her, except with his knees, but she seemed to know her way home. He would have to be careful that she did not wander in future, Abe thought. Farmers did not take kindly to other people's animals trespassing on their grazing land. It was lucky there was a mist tonight. No one could have seen her. He sighed with relief and sat, slackly hunched, in the hollow of her back.

Lulled by her steady motion, he was nodding, on the edge of sleep, when she stopped still. He stiffened, yawning and rubbing his knuckles in his eyes. He grumbled, 'Git *on*, Whitey. I'm starved cold . . .'

But she didn't move. Her ears were pricked up and pointing straight ahead.

'There's nothing there,' Abe said, but as soon as he spoke he knew this was not true. He could hear the drumming hooves again, not loud this time but insistent and, terrifyingly, not only outside his head but inside it, too. Frantic, he beat his frozen feet on the old mare's sides. She began to move, reluctantly at first, and then breaking into an untidy trot. 'Giddup,' Abe urged her in a whisper, but she seemed unable to go faster. Unable – or unwilling? Could she hear the drumming too? She shied suddenly – at nothing, it seemed. Abe looked up and just ahead of him, at the very edge of Gibbet Wood, the mist lifted and he saw – for the rest of his life he swore to it – the horse standing there with its terrible rider, motionless, headless, staring. Then the mist came down and horse and rider vanished like a dream. Abe cried out, once, and his voice echoed back from the mist as from a wall. The white mare gathered herself beneath him and then stretched out in a slow, clumsy canter.

Abe lay on her back, half-fainting, and she carried him safely home.

CHAPTER EIGHT

SAM and Rose did not doubt that Abe had seen the Headless Hunter. His pale, awed face as he told them, was sufficient evidence of truth. 'I'd have *died*,' Rose said 'Oh Abe, how will you ever dare go past there again?'

'Course, it might've been a tree, things look funny sometimes in the mist,' Sam said, but he did not really believe it, nor was he fooled by Abe's parade of indifference.

'Oh, I shan't tek no notice,' he said in answer to Rose's question, but for the whole of that day he was listless and quiet, not just in class which was normal enough, but also during break and the dinner hour. He stood leaning against the wall of the playground and staring into space, his mouth slightly open. He did not even come to life when they discussed their exploit of the night before.

That the tree planting had had some effect, they were sure. But *what* effect, exactly? Miss Pennyfather appeared abstracted and listless, rather like Abe. Her discipline was much milder than usual – indeed, it was almost non-existent. She seemed not to notice when her class shouted and giggled and threw paper darts. When Jim Walsh removed one of the newts from the aquarium on the window sill and slid it neatly down the neck of the girl who sat in front of him, Miss Pennyfather roused herself sufficiently to give him a black mark, but that was all. No one else got a black mark, no one else was sent to the Headmaster. Miss Pennyfather's thoughts seemed elsewhere. For much of the day she stared, as she had always reproached her pupils for doing, out of the window. In an odd way, Sam began to feel uncomfortable.

Once, when he looked up from his desk, he found Miss Pennyfather watching him. She turned red and looked away.

'I wish I'd been there when she saw it this morning,' Rose sighed. 'I bet she was *sick*.'

'I wish I'd been there too,' Sam said. 'Don't you, Abe?'

Abe shifted his position against the wall. 'Don't I what?'

'Wish you could've been there this morning when she saw the tree?'

'Dono. Oh – I suppose so,' Abe muttered.

His lassitude persisted. When school was over, he slipped away without saying good-bye. Sam and Rose knew why, though neither spoke of it: Abe did not want to be drawn into some game which might last until dusk fell. He wanted to get home in full daylight.

'We couldn't have done much, anyway,' Sam said. 'It's going to rain.'

It did rain before they got home, sharp, spiky rain that had hail in it. Sam picked up one hailstone big as a marble but the find did not excite him as much as it would usually have done. He felt curiously subdued and, from the uninterested way Rose glanced at the hailstone, he could tell she did, too.

Tiredness was part of it, of course. They yawned all through tea.

'You can't be tired, surely?' Mrs Peach said. 'You had that lovely long sleep, last night!'

When they went up to bed just as early as they had done the evening before, she was worried.

'They must be sickening for something,' she told Mr Peach.

'Angling for a day off school,' said Mr Peach, who had a naturally sour view of human nature.

Once in bed, Sam's tiredness mysteriously vanished. He lay miserably awake, listening to the hail clatter against the window.

He couldn't quite locate the source of his misery. He fell to thinking of Miss Pennyfather. It was, really, very unlikely indeed that she thought the tree had grown up in the night like a magic beanstalk. She must have known Sam had played a trick on her. But it was quite a *funny* trick, Sam pleaded – almost as if he were being accused of something in a court of law. Yes, but perhaps *she* hadn't thought it so funny! She was not a person to laugh much. She had thought it kind of Sam to give her a present – she had said so – and now she knew it hadn't been kind. He had only done it so he could play this trick on her.

Seen in this light, it didn't seem funny at all. Sam twisted in bed and tried to think of something else but it didn't work: he kept on thinking of Miss Pennyfather. Sam groaned and pressed his knuckles into his eyes until the sparks flew, red and green and gold. Then he tried holding his breath and counting slowly in his head. He made himself think of the horse-chesnut tree on the football ground and made plans to go there with Rose tomorrow and get a good sackful. The chestnuts were almost ready: the burrs were yellowing, the prickles hardening, and inside the burr the glossy brown nut would be ready – for stringing, or stroking, or just for collecting ...

But it was no good. Miss Pennyfather's face, turning that awful, slow red when she looked at him, was still there in his mind's eye, and he couldn't get rid of it.

He realized that he never wanted to see her again and then, that there was no way he could achieve this except through death. He didn't particularly want to die at this moment, but the thought that he might, provided the diversion he had been looking for. How sorry everyone would be!

Suppose he was thrown from Abe's horse and struck his head on a stone! He would be brought home, dying. They would lay him in his bed and his mother would smooth his hair back, tears in her eyes, begging him to forgive her for all the unkind things she had done to him. There was a slight difficulty here as Mrs Peach was never unkind, only sometimes unnoticing. Mr Peach was a more suitable subject. He often said unkind and cutting things and last week he had deprived Sam of his pocket money for being rude to Mrs Mountjoy. Sam pictured his father on his knees beside his bed, saying, 'Speak to me, Sam. Oh, my boy, speak to me . . .'

The water came into Sam's eyes and mouth and he had to swallow hard and blink.

It was then that he realized someone was really crying. Muffled sobs came from Rose's room across the landing. Sam lay still for a minute, listening; then he got up, hitched his pyjama trousers, and padded in to her.

She was lying on her stomach, the pillow over her head. Sam tried to move it and she struck out at him. 'Oh – go *away* . . .'

Sam retreated to the end of the bed, wrapped the eiderdown round him and waited. Rose sat up, sniffing. Her hair stood up damp and spiky and her eyes and nose were swollen.

'Are you crying about Miss Pennyfather?' Sam asked.

She shook her head, looking surprised.

'What's the matter, then?'

'I was thinking about my parents. I don't know why. I just felt miserable and then I started to think about them and then I started crying.' Her lips began to quiver. 'And then I just couldn't stop.'

'I didn't think you missed them. Not *so* much, I mean.'

'Most of the time I don't. I mean I like being here with you and Abe and being in a gang. I've never been in a gang before. But sometimes I wish I could just see them and then come back again . . .' She fumbled under the pillow for her handkerchief, and blew her nose. She went on shakily. 'Auntie never kisses me good night. My mother always did.'

'Mum's not used to girls,' Sam said. 'I mean she's only had a boy and boys don't go in for kissing much. I could remind her if you like – sort of suggest that you'd like her to . . .'

Rose shook her head. 'No. Thank you all the same.' She lay down and stared at the ceiling.

Sam tried to think of something to cheer her up. 'There's a circus coming next week. It comes every year about this time. They have it on the field. It's quite a good circus and they have a Zoo as well. You only pay threepence for the Zoo but the circus seats are more. I expect Mum'll pay for us to go.'

'My father says circuses are barbaric,' Rose said in a very sleepy voice.

Sam was going to say that what Rose's father thought hardly mattered, as he wasn't there, and then he realized that this was just what Rose was crying about, so he held his tongue. He tried to think of something else that might make Rose feel happier. 'We could go chestnut-ing tomorrow if you like,' he said, but she didn't answer.

She had gone suddenly and peacefully to sleep.

Next day, they went to the chestnut tree in the dinner hour. They threw sticks up, and soon the burrs were lying thick on the ground. They began splitting the burrs and sorting out the brown, marbled nuts. Rose took part in this occupation, but without much real interest. She was silent and withdrawn.

Abe, who had recovered his own spirits since yesterday, asked her what was the matter.

'Nothing,' Rose said.

77

'She's fretting about her parents,' Sam explained.

Rose did not deny this. She sat listlessly on the grass, her lap full of conkers.

Abe looked at her curiously. 'Ain't they coming back for you?' he asked suddenly.

'Course they're coming back. She's just a bit homesick,' Sam said.

Abe went on splitting burrs with his finger nail Then he said, unexpectedly, 'Mine didn't come back for me. My Mum and Dad went off to Australia and they said they'd send for me, but they never did. My Gran reckons they never meant to . . .'

Rose's eyes grew round. They were the same colour as the conkers, Sam thought. 'Oh *Abe*,' she said.

'They never wrote, neither.'

'I've had letters,' Rose said.

'D'you know when they're coming back, though?'

Rose shook her head.

'Well, then . . .' Abe shrugged his shoulders fatalistically.

'They'll come to fetch me soon,' Rose said, but she sounded uncertain.

'Course they will,' Sam said, to comfort her, although he was beginning to have doubts himself. But she paid no heed to him. Her brown, troubled eyes were fixed on Abe.

'D'you really think . . .' she began, and then swallowed hard.

Abe shifted uneasily. '*I* dono, do I? All I know is, parents get fed up. My Mum used to like me all right but mebbe once she went off, she felt different. Absence don't always make the heart grow fonder, that's what my Gran says.'

Rose was silent. She fondled a conker with her thumb. Then she said, 'If I could just fly out and see them. Maybe your mother would have felt different if she'd seen you.'

'Mebbe,' Abe said indifferently.

'It costs a lot to get to America,' Sam said.

'How much?'

''Bout a hundred pounds, I should think.'

Abe whistled gloomily. Gloom settled on them all. Rose had not had a letter for more than a week. Even if there was only the slenderest possible chance that her parents were likely to behave like Abe's, it was enough to make her despair. Abe was quite sure all parents were the same, given the chance they would be glad to be rid of their children; but, watching Rose, he wished he had never opened his mouth. Even Sam, who could not imagine that his parents would ever abandon *him*, could think of nothing cheering to say. He did his best, sorting the conkers into three piles and giving the best ones to Rose. 'Here's a beauty! Look, you can have this one!' he kept saying, but suddenly Rose lost patience and cried out, 'Oh, don't be stupid! I hate conkers!' and bursting into tears, got up and walked off.

Sam ran after her but she turned away, the tears falling down her cheeks. 'Go away, leave me alone, can't you? I hate you!'

'Leave her be,' Abe advised and they watched her wander crying across the football field and into the deserted school playground.

Abe said, 'I reckon she ought to fly out. How c'n we get a hundred pounds, Sam?'

'I've got twenty-five pounds in the post office,' Sam said. 'But my Mum's got the book. Anyway, we need more than that.' He thought for a while. 'We could steal it, I s'pose.'

'Where from? My Gran's got some money under her mattress,' Abe said. 'But I doubt it 'ud be enough.'

Full of melancholy, they collected the best of the conkers and stuffed their pockets. The school bell began to clang across the field, and, sighing, they made their slow way towards another long afternoon's boredom. At the edge of the field, Percy Mountjoy appeared from behind a tree.

'Hullo, Sam,' he said.

Sam was too dispirited to be rude to him. ''Lo,' he said weakly.

'You been collecting conkers?' Percy asked. He was wearing grey linen shorts buttoning on to a blue shirt, his pale hair was licked down dark with water and fastened with – of all things! – a girl's tortoise-shell hair slide. Abe and Sam looked at him with distaste.

'How old are you?' Abe asked.

'Seven, going on eight. Would you like to see my double one?' He held out a beautiful nut with the burr split neatly open and showing the soft white inside and the two perfect, glossy nuts. 'You can have it if you like,' he said.

Both boys looked at the nut enviously, but made no move to take it.

'Don't you want it?' Percy said in a disappointed voice. He put it back in his pocket. 'I'm going to the circus on Monday,' he said importantly. 'Are you going to the circus, Sam?'

'I expect so.' A thought struck him. 'Why haven't you gone back to school?'

'I'm not going back for another week. I've had a nasty cold.'

Abe and Sam looked at each other. 'Only babies stay at home because they've got colds,' Sam said.

Percy's pale cheeks went pink. 'I'm not a baby. Can I play with you after tea?'

They hesitated. Percy was innocent and silly as a baby duck and they were both too despondent, at this moment, to be deliberately unkind to him. But the decision was taken out of their hands.

'*Percy.*' Mrs Mountjoy was leaning out of the window of her house. '**PERCY**! Come here this minute!'

Percy glanced over his shoulder at his mother and turned back to the boys. '*Can* I?' he pleaded urgently.

'Your Mam wants you jus' now,' Abe said and, taking Percy by the shoulders, gave him a little push towards the road.

This gesture was misunderstood by Mrs Mountjoy who shouted in a paroxysm of rage that Abe was to let her Percy go, now, this very minute! 'Don't you dare put your hands on *him*,' she screamed. 'You dreadful, vulgar boy!'

Abe whipped his hands back as if he had been stung. Percy hurried across the road without looking and only just missed being knocked down by an old man on a bicycle. This near-accident produced a fresh torrent of abuse from Mrs Mountjoy who threatened Abe with the police, with his Headmaster, and with her own revenge, if only she could get her hands on *him*.

'Come away,' Sam urged, as Abe stood staring at his enemy and going first red, then white.

But Abe did not move until Mrs Mountjoy vacated the window and appeared at her front door. She drew Percy inside the house and shut the door with an angry slam. Abe drew a long, quivering sigh and followed Sam silently, back to school.

He did not speak until they were at the door of the classroom. Then he caught Sam's sleeve and held him back. 'I got an idea,' he whispered. 'It's a good idea, 'cause it'll do two things – get our own back and make some money. Want to hear?'

Sam nodded and Abe put his mouth to his ear. 'We c'n kidnap Percy Mountjoy,' he said.

CHAPTER NINE

'WE got to *plan*,' Sam said. 'Most people get caught doing things because they haven't planned properly.'

It was late afternoon, at the cob-nut tree. Although Sam and Rose were so excited they had barely been able to swallow any tea, their faces were grave now: this was too important a project to be taken lightly.

Only Abe was inclined to be casual. ''S quite easy,' he said. 'We jus' kidnap him an' then we hide him an' then we send a letter about the ransom.'

Sam sighed, shaking his head. 'That's what I *mean*. S'no good just *saying* all that. You got to work everything out first. First thing, we got to find somewhere safe to hide him – somewhere he'll be good and safe.'

'My Gran's going off, Monday,' Abe said. 'She's going to her sister over at Long Broughton, an' she'll stay till Friday, most like. So he c'n stay up with me for a bit – no one 'ud think of looking up at me Gran's place.'

Sam and Rose glanced at each other. It seemed strange to think of Mrs Tanner having relations like other people.

'Only thing is, we'll have to git a bit of extra food,' Abe said. 'Me Gran'll leave a bit, tins and bread an' stuff, but t'wont be enough for him too.'

'We'll get chocolate and things like peanuts,' Sam said. 'Iron rations. We get them this week-end and hide 'em up in one of the shacks before your Gran goes off. I get ninepence, Saturday. How much money you got, Rose?'

'Five and sevenpence. And I know what to do about the letter. What you do is get a newspaper and cut out the words you want and stick them on to a piece of brown paper with glue. Then no one can find out where it comes from. If you write it, you see, the police can trace your handwriting.'

The two boys looked at her. 'How'd you think of that?' Abe asked, astonished.

'When I was in Paris, there was a boy kidnapped and it was all in the papers. And there was even a picture of this piece of brown paper. The way they caught the kidnappers was that the paper had come off a parcel. It was an inside bit, and when they looked carefully they could see the address where the parcel was sent – it had sort of pressed through.'

'We'll have to get a new piece – or a big envelope 'ud do,' Sam said. 'And we'll want a newspaper and some scissors and some glue. And then we'll have to work out what we want to say.'

'Hand over the money or else ...' Abe said. He laughed suddenly and, getting up, turned three perfect cart wheels, one after the other.

'Or else you won't see your son alive again,' Rose said in a solemn, blood-curdling voice.

'The penalty is DEATH,' Abe chanted and drew his finger across his thoat with a bubbling sound. He dropped limply on to the grass and lay there, mouth open, eyes staring up at the sky.

Rose giggled.

'Oh, stop mucking about,' Sam said crossly. 'This isn't a *game*. You got to be serious.'

His voice was so stern that Abe sat up, shame-faced. 'What do we put in the letter then, Sam?'

Sam frowned. 'I'll have to work that out. We'll do the letter over the week-end and get the food all ready. But that's not the most important part. We got somewhere to hide him, but how are we going to get him there? I mean that's what we got to think about.' He put on a heavily sarcastic voice. 'You can't just go up to him and say Come along, Percy, we're going to kidnap you and hold you to ransom! It's no good talking about what we're going to do when we've *got* him. We got to get him first.'

'We could chloroform him,' Rose said. 'You can get some chloroform from Uncle's shop and put it on a rag or something and then jump out at him and hold it over his face.'

Sam stared, horrified. 'Oh, I can, can I? And suppose I give him too much. Suppose he *dies*.'

'Don't give him too much then,' Rose said. She lifted her chin and the colour came into her face. 'You're being an awful spoilsport, Sam. You scared, or something?'

'Course I'm not scared,' Sam said indignantly. 'Only I got a bit more sense than you have, that's all. All this talk of chloroform and killing, it's just silly.'

'Scared,' Rose said complacently.

'I'm not.'

'You are, then.'

'All right. If you say I'm scared, you can just get on and do it all by yourself.'

'All right, we will. And I suppose you'll go and tell on us, too!'

Sam gave her a look of withering scorn, turned his back and walked away, down the field. When Abe called out to him he slowed his footsteps a little but kept on, not looking back, until they panted up behind him.

'I'm sorry,' Rose said. 'Of course you won't tell. I only said that to be horrid.'

'We can't do it without you,' Abe said. 'You're much better at planning than we are.'

They both appeared serious and penitent. 'All right,' Sam said grudgingly. 'All right, then. Only I'm not going to get any chloroform or anything dangerous like that.'

Abe nodded his head. 'We won't do no chloroforming, Sam, if you say so. But I reckon there's no need. Percy'll do anything you say, won't he? You've only got to git hold of him when his Mam's not about an' say you want him to come an' play. Then you bring him up to my place an' if he 'on't stay, we can tie him up.'

'Bind him and gag him,' Rose said with relish.

'There's no need to gag him, who's to hear him up there?' Sam was slightly shocked at Rose's appetite for violence. He was not normally squeamish but as Rose and Abe seemed to have assumed that the main burden of the operation was to be borne by him, he was inclined to be extra solemn and responsible. He was also readier to see snags than they were.

'I don't see how I'll ever get him by himself,' he complained gloomily. '*She's* always there.'

'What about the circus?' Abe suggested. 'He said he was going Monday. He'll sit at the front with the children and she'll sit at the back.'

'Only if it's the same as last year.'

'It's always the same,' Abe said. 'Benches at the front where the children sit, an' near the benches there's always a loose place under the tent where you c'n git through without paying. We'll scout around and find out where 'tis and you tell him to git through there 'stead of going out the ordinary way, and his Mum'll never notice.'

'Suppose he won't come?'

'Course he'll come. You jus' tell him the tale, Sam, an' he'll come right enough.'

Sam gave the tiniest of sighs. 'I suppose so,' he said.

Sam had often thought of kidnapping someone – a rich heiress, say – and holding her to ransom in a cave somewhere. She would cry and be scared at first, but after a while she would settle down and cook his food and mend his clothes while he lay low in the hills. But now the victim was named and the deed imminent, his courage dwindled; indeed, if Rose had shown the least sign of doubt, it might have evaporated altogether.

Unfortunately, Rose had no doubts. Perhaps this was because her own part in the kidnapping was to be less central than Sam's. When they discussed it later that evening, whispering in her darkened room, she said they must be very careful not to be seen together on the fateful day. 'We don't want people to think we're a gang,' she explained. The best thing would be for Abe to be absent from school on Monday. They could tell Miss Pennyfather he had gone to Long Broughton with his Gran. And she would sit with the other girls at the circus. 'T' would be much better if you kidnapped Percy on your own,' she said. 'Abe can wait outside somewhere and help you tie him up, and I can come along later.'

This did nothing to cheer Sam up. He went to bed and lay awake, tossing and turning. Apart from his general apprehension, there was a nagging feeling at the back of his mind that there was something quite dreadfully wrong with the whole plan, but he could not put a finger on it.

Miraculously, when morning came, all his fears had vanished. Monday was a long way off – four days! Anything could happen in four days, and meanwhile they had a great many things to do.

They laid out all the money they had between them. They spent sixpence on glue and the rest on chocolate and packets of mixed nuts and raisins and half a dozen sherbet dabs. Sam wanted to buy baked beans, his own favourite food, but Rose said it would be foolish to buy that sort of thing. 'People would think it funny, children buying groceries. They'd guess there was something up,' she said.

'But we don't want him to starve,' Sam objected. 'And you can't just live on chocolates and raisins.'

'Explorers often do,' Rose said. 'Anyway, Abe'll give him some of his food and some goat's milk. But we can get hold of a few other things if you like. And warm clothes. We ought to get him something warm to wear, like a jersey or something.'

'That's funny,' Mrs Peach said on Saturday morning. 'I could have sworn I bought a fruit cake yesterday. And surely there ought to be a few tins of baked beans?' She looked doubtfully at Sam and Rose. 'You children been in the larder?'

'No, Auntie.'

'I expect you just thought you'd bought a cake, you know what you are,' Sam said.

'I'm sure I *did*, though. Oh well,' – Mrs Peach sighed – 'maybe you're right, Sam. There's another thing I meant to ask you – what was it, now?' She rumpled her hair and stared out of the window as if she hoped to read the answer in the sky. 'Oh, I know, whatever happened to that old football jersey of yours, Sam? I was going to mend it up yesterday, but I couldn't find it anywhere.'

Rose said, 'Don't you remember, Auntie? You gave it to the Scouts when they came last week. For their jumble sale.'

'Did I? I don't remember . . . .' Mrs Peach sighed again, 'I'll forget my own head, one day.'

'Where are you going with that newspaper, Sam?' Mr Peach said on Sunday afternoon. 'I've not looked at it yet.'

'It's last week's, Dad,' Sam said. 'I want it to make paper boats.'

'I didn't imagine you wanted to read it,' Mr Peach said in

a sneering voice. He found his newspaper behind the cushion of his chair, settled his spectacles on his nose, and opened it. Then he lowered the pages, peered over the top of his spectacles and added, 'Bit old for paper boats, aren't you?'

'I've never made boats,' Rose said. 'Sam said he'd show me.'

'Got the glue, Sam?'

'In my pocket. Oh *Lord*, the top's come off.'

Sam produced a half empty bottle of glue, turned his pocket inside out and tried to clean out the mess with a handful of grass.

'What a mess,' Rose said. 'You are *messy*, Sam '

'T'was a rotten old cork,' Sam muttered. 'I've half a mind to take it back and tell them.'

'That 'ud be silly, just calling attention,' Abe told him severely. 'And your Mam'll wonder what you bin up to when she sees that jacket, won't she?'

'Can't help that.' Sam went on, scrubbing away with the grass but without success. The grass stuck to the glue and then the mixture of glue-and-grass transferred itself not only to Sam's fingers but also, mysteriously, to his face and hair. By the time he had abandoned the attempt to clean out the pocket, there seemed to be three times more glue on his clothes and his person than there had ever been in the bottle. 'I'll just have to lose the beastly thing,' Sam said, and, taking off his jacket, threw it despairingly on the grass.

Without it, he shivered. Though they were sitting in the lee of one of the shacks, it was cold up by the old mine. Black cloud shadows rushed across the green hills. 'We can't do the letter here, that's a sure thing,' Abe said, as he unfolded last Sunday's newspaper and the sheets flapped like sails in the westerly gale.

They crawled inside the shack. It was dark and smelt of

mould and rats. Rose looked suspiciously into the corners before taking a large envelope and a pair of nail scissors out of her pocket. Abe spread the newspaper on the dirt floor and looked at Sam expectantly. 'What we going to say, Sam?'

'Depends what words we find,' Sam said. 'Something like, Your Son Has Been Kidnapped by A Dangerous Gang. That would do for a start.'

They crouched over the newspaper for a long time, in silence. It was surprisingly difficult to find the words they wanted. Certainly, the words 'kidnapped' and 'dangerous' seemed totally absent from this Sunday newspaper. 'We'll just have to leave a space and print them in pencil,' Sam said.

They found 'son' and 'has' and 'been' and 'by' but the words were too small, once they were cut out, for even Rose's neat fingers to handle easily. The paper had picked up loose dirt from the floor which got mixed up with the glue; by the time she had finished trying to stick the words on to the envelope, they were only just legible, and Rose herself was as messily sticky as Sam had been.

'Perhaps headlines 'ud be easier,' Sam suggested, but the only one he could find that seemed even faintly relevant was SWIFT ACTION IS NECESSARY TO SAVE LIFE.

'What's that mean?' Abe said.

'Well – *here* it's all about the awful traffic somewhere, but in our letter it 'ud mean that if they don't pay up quickly, he'll be killed.'

'Don't make much sense to me.'

'What about PROFESSIONAL CRIMINALS MUST BE RESTRAINED SAYS BISHOP,' Rose asked.

'What's bishops got to do with it.'

'I didn't mean we'd use all of it,' Rose explained. 'Only PROFESSIONAL CRIMINALS. I mean we could end up, saying saying We Are Professional Criminals.'

'WE ARE DESPERATE MEN 'ud be better,' Sam said.

'We haven't got that, have we, Clever Dick?' Rose snapped.

'I don't think what we have got's much use,' Sam said. He was beginning to feel as if he had been sitting in the same scrooged up position for hours and hours. 'I got cramp,' he complained, but Rose took no notice. She cut and glued in silence, the pink tip of her tongue protruding from her mouth. 'Give me the pencil, Sam,' she said, and then, a minute later, 'Look, is this all right?'

'I think it's a mess,' Sam said candidly. 'I mean it just looks as if kids have done it.'

YOUR son has been KIDNAPPED by

PROFESSIONAL CRIMINALS.

SWIFT ACTION IS NECESSARY

TO SAVE HIS LIFE.

Rose looked disappointed and Abe said quickly, 'T'aint as bad as that, Sam. But t'aint right, neither. It's no good just saying you want a hundred pound – you got to say where *she's* got to bring it. An' that needs a lotta thinking over.' He stood up and stretched. 'I vote we give over. I'm starved cold.'

Rose and Sam were perfectly willing. Composing the ransom letter was a much more tedious business than they had ever imagined it could be and they were bored as well as frozen. They scrumpled the newspaper up and stuffed it in a corner of the shack with the envelope and weighted it all down with a large stone.

'Let's go down and see how the circus is getting on,' Sam said.

Most of the children of Castle Stoke were on the football ground, watching the men put up the Big Top. Four vans with trailers were parked at the edge of the field. Thomas Gale's Travelling Circus and Menagerie, was painted on their sides. There were three caravans and five piebald horses with long tails tethered beside them.

'It's a very small circus, isn't it?' Rose said, but Abe and Sam took no notice of her.

'They've got a new lion,' Sam said, pointing out one of the vans that carried a newly-painted poster of a savage, snarling beast leaping through a flaming hoop.

But only the picture was new. Peeping through the entrance of the trailer, they saw the same old lion as last year, stretched out limp and mangy on the floor of his cage.

'Marcus. The only Tamed Man-Eating Lion in the World,' Sam read out from the poster. 'D'you think he really *is* a man-eater, Abe?'

'You're going the right way to find out, laddie,' said one of the circus men, coming up behind them and pushing them away from the door. 'You've got no business poking round the vans. If you got in there, old Marcus 'ud crunch you up, easy as apples.'

He grinned, showing gold teeth. Sam said, '*Last* year we could look at the animals.'

'Only if you paid. Get along now.'

'*I ast* year it was free on Sunday,' Sam said.

The man narrowed his eyes and looked angry, but only

for a minute. Then he laughed. 'Not the lion, lad, nor the tigers. Only the wolves and the bear is free. They're not performers.' He jerked his head. 'Over there.'

The Menagerie smelt. It was a long trailer with a narrow corridor down one side and double-barred cages on the other. In one, a comfortable-looking brown bear with ragged claws dozed quietly in a corner, not to be roused, even when they threw chestnuts at him. In the middle cage were two female wolves and in the last, a big dog wolf paced up and down, shoulders rubbing against the bars. When he came to one end of his cage he jerked his head up, swung round, and loped back to the other.

'He looks just like a dog,' Rose said.

The wolf stopped suddenly and stood still. The thick fur rose on his shoulders like a ruff, and the children saw that a small trap door on the far side of his cage was slightly open. A long, whippy stick poked slowly through the aperture and waved about the floor. They rushed out of the trailer and round the side to find Jim Walsh on his knees, holding the other end of the stick. 'They left a bolt undone feedin' time,' he said. 'It's super – you c'n make him dance . . .'

They went back inside the menagerie and watched as the big wolf did, indeed, seem to dance, jumping stiff-legged over and round the waving stick. From time to time he got hold of the end and shook the stick with a growl that was not like a dog's growl but deeper and more menacing. It was a marvellously frightening sensation when you had hold of the other end of the stick, as the children discovered: Jim Walsh gave them each a turn so that he could see the show from inside.

Sam was waving the stick when Mrs Peach appeared. He did not notice her until she shouted at him and grabbed his shoulder, wrenching him backwards so that he let go the stick and tumbled over on the muddy ground.

It was the first time Sam had ever seen his mother really angry. Her eyes snapped and she was quivering. 'Tormenting dumb animals!' she cried. 'Oh, I'm ashamed of you, Sam. We'll see what your father has to say about it, when I get you home!'

CHAPTER TEN

Mr Peach had more to say about Sam's missing jacket than his teasing of the wolf.

'Downright criminal carelessness,' he raged at breakfast when Sam admitted his loss. 'And it's not the first time!' With a certain grim pleasure, he listed the articles Sam had mislaid or maltreated recently. It made an imposing total. Sam listened with downcast eyes: he knew from experience that breakfast was not the time to answer Mr Peach back.

'I don't know what to do with you, though I know what *my* father would have done to me! He would have given me a good thrashing!' Mr Peach paused effectively before adding that he did not approve of corporal punishment.

Sam said nothing.

'Well, what do *you* think I should do with you, Sam?' Mr Peach asked.

'I don't know, Dad.'

This mild answer seemed to annoy Mr Peach. Red patches appeared on his cheeks.

'Don't you? Well, I do!' Mr Peach poured himself another cup of tea, took his spectacles out of his pocket and adjusted them on his nose. He opened his newspaper slowly to prolong the agony. 'You will not go to the circus this afternoon,' he announced.

'Oh, Uncle,' Rose protested, but Mr Peach only rustled his paper and began to read the leading article.

'What are we going to do?' Rose said, as soon as they were out of the house.

94

'Dono.'

'Shall I ask Auntie to get him to change his mind?'

'T'wouldn't be no good.'

They walked down the town in silence, Rose gloomy, Sam rather less so. If he could not go to the circus, there was small chance of kidnapping Percy today.

Suddenly a black cat streaked across their path and disappeared in an alley. Sam stopped dead and turned round three times.

'What are you doing?' Rose asked, surprised.

'Putting off the bad luck. Didn't you know you had to do that?' Sam sighed and shook his head. 'Don't always work, though. P'raps it's a warning about Percy. P'raps it means we oughtn't to do it, after all. Not *today*, anyway,' he added hastily.

'Why ever not, Sam?'

'Well – it might be dangerous, after seeing that cat.' Sam thought that Rose was remarkably ignorant in some ways. Although for most of the time he only half-believed in the danger of bad omens, he saw how he could make use of this one. 'Black cats are the worst thing of all,' he explained solemnly. 'Worse than seeing one crow or the back of an ambulance. You spit if you see those but it don't always work.'

Looking slyly at his cousin to see how she was taking it, he went on to tell the story of a boy he knew who had seen both these things, one after the other, and, though he spat on the ground seven times, had fallen off a wall and broken his leg within the hour.

Rose was suitably impressed – or appeared to be, anyway. Perhaps now Monday was actually here, she had been growing faint-hearted herself. 'Maybe we ought to wait until we see a lucky sign,' she said thoughtfully. 'What's lucky, Sam?'

'Don't you know? Oh – a white horse, o'course, or stepping in horse muck, or a black cat, *sometimes*. If it sits down in front of you or walks straight on ahead.'

Rose looked about her. 'I can't see any of those things just at the moment, can you?' she said, in a tone of artificial surprise.

'No,' Sam admitted.

'Then we ought to wait till we do, I suppose.'

'I reckon so,' Sam said.

They walked on, both much lighter in heart, but slightly constrained by the knowledge that they had, really, funked the desperate thing they had planned to do. Each of them was wondering what the other was thinking and what Abe would say when he knew they were not going to kidnap Percy after all. Neither of them wanted to be the first to mention Abe, who, as Rose had suggested, was not coming to school today. This evening, when the circus began, he was to wait for them up in the cob nut field.

Poor Abe, Rose thought. He would be dreadfully let down. Waiting up there, alone in the cold and the dark, and all for nothing! Suddenly she could bear this thought no longer and burst out, 'We got to let Abe know, Sam. Just as soon as we can.'

'I can't let him know till after school, can I?' Sam said. 'S'no good going looking for him in the dinner hour. He might be anywhere.' Rose's face fell. 'I'll go soon as you've gone to the circus,' Sam consoled her. 'Then he won't be kept waiting long.'

Now that the kidnapping idea had been safely shelved, the fact that he was actually going to miss the circus came home to him properly. He had looked forward to it with such anticipation! 'It'll be the first time I've missed it,' he lamented. 'The first time in my whole life!'

Rose was touched by the bleak misery on his face. 'If

Uncle won't let you go, then *I* won't go either,' she said, and squeezed his hand.

But Mr Peach refused to allow this loyal sacrifice. He wouldn't consider it for a minute, he said at tea-time, setting his long jaw and looking coldly at his son and his niece. Why, it was part of Sam's punishment that he should suffer it by himself. In fact, to press the point home, he was to escort his cousin down to the football field and watch her go into the circus tent with her schoolfellows while he remained outside, an outcast, alone . . .

'And I am *not* being unfair,' Mr Peach trumpeted. Glaring, he picked up his coat and went off, back to his shop.

'*I* think he's unfair,' Rose said as they walked to the field. 'I wish you could come, Sam. I shan't enjoy it without you – not one little bit.'

'You'll enjoy it all right once you get there,' Sam said. 'It 'ud be downright silly not to, really. I mean, t'wouldn't do *me* any good if you didn't, would it? So you might as well.'

In spite of this high-minded speech, Sam felt very forlorn as he watched Rose join the long queue of children shuffling their way towards the opening in the tent. Various friends called out to him. 'What's the matter? An't you coming, Sam?'

'No,' Sam said. 'No – there's no special reason. I'm just not coming.' And then, more defiantly, 'Who wants to go to an ole circus? Circuses are just for kids,' but after a while the back of his throat began to prickle and he had to turn away so that no one should see the tears in his eyes.

Once they had all gone in, he stood near to the tent flap and sniffed the beautiful, musty smell of sawdust and animals. Then the twanging music began and gusty outbursts of laughter, making him feel even more forsaken and desperate. They were all enjoying themselves without a thought for him; nobody cared that he had been left outside, alone; nobody loved him; his father hated the sight of him and probably wished he had never been born. The best thing, clearly, would be to go right away where no one would have to set eyes on him again! Yes – that's what he would do, he thought, and once he had gone for ever, perhaps they would all be sorry! The tears began to spurt out of his eyes.

A handful of newcomers rushed up to the paybox and glanced at him curiously. Sam turned his back and walked round the bulging sides of the tent, into darkness. As he walked, he kicked savagely at the tufty grass. He would go this minute, up into the cold bleak hills and die of starvation! But first he would go and find Abe and tell him what he planned to do. Perhaps Abe would come too, he thought suddenly, his spirits lifting; they would run away together; they would live like guerilla fighters up in the hills, they would shelter in shepherd's huts and caves; they would drink from hill streams and catch fish, or steal a sheep and roast it whole on a spit over a fire ...

Sam dried his eyes on his sleeve and set off across the field.

He had only gone a few yards when a particularly loud gale of laughter arrested him. He turned and looked back. The big tent was threaded with gold at the worn seams and, in one place, there was quite a wedge of light where the bottom of the tent met the ground. In this place the tent flapped a little, as if a peg had worked loose.

Sam darted back. The peg *was* loose – one tug and it was out, leaving a space clear for a boy to wriggle underneath. Sam lay on his stomach and worked his way forward on his elbows. When his shoulders were inside he lifted his head cautiously and gasped at his wonderful good luck.

He couldn't have found a better place: he was right beside the wooden run where the animals came in to the ring. The benches where the children sat stopped a good yard away from the wooden barrier and Sam had a clear view of a short, fat clown in baggy trousers who was climbing on a chair in order to empty a bucket of water over the head of the ringmaster who stood with his back to him. A rustle of giggling crept round the audience as the ringmaster waved his arms and cracked his whip and talked about the wonderful act they were going to see in a minute – two tigers and Marcus, the man-eating lion. The small fat clown lost his balance and fell off the chair on to his back but managed to save the bucket of water from spilling by catching it on his feet. A few children began clapping but he got up carefully and put his finger to his lips, hushing them to silence. He climbed on to the chair again. The ringmaster went on talking. The small, fat clown held the bucket of water high. The ringmaster lifted his whip and swept it behind his head, neatly tipping the bucket so that the water emptied over the head of the small clown who stood there, holding the bucket while the water flowed down into his baggy trousers which began to swell up and up, like a balloon. The children laughed, the trousers swelled. Sam began to laugh too; his ribs hurt as he bounced up and down on the hard ground. Suddenly the clown's trousers fell off him, leaving him standing in long, red and white striped underpants. Sam let out a great shriek and tried to stuff his jersey sleeve in his mouth to stifle it.

But he was too late. Several of the children sitting on the nearest bench turned round. None of them would give him away deliberately, Sam knew, but they were small children who might easily attract attention by too much mysterious giggling and head-turning. He prepared to wriggle backwards at once but luckily they were so taken up with the clown that they only glanced at him for a minute, their eyes blurred with laughter, before they all turned their attention back to the ring.

All but one, that is.

'Sam,' said a voice, 'Sam *Peach*.'

To Sam's horror, Percy was sitting on the bench, third from the end. He had turned completely round and was looking at Sam with joyful wonder.

'Ssh,' Sam hissed, trying to smile in a friendly way and frown a warning at the same time.

'What are you making that funny face for?' Percy asked. 'Have you hurt yourself?'

'No,' Sam whispered. 'Don't *shout*.'

'I'm not shouting,' Percy said, in a good, healthy bellow. 'What are you doing there? On the *ground*?'

'Sitting in the best seats, what d'you think?' Sam said savagely.

'But you're not ...'

With a groan of rage, Sam jabbed his elbows into the ground, shot himself backwards and let the tent edge fall. He stood up, rubbing his stiff arms and feeling disgruntled: he had hoped to stay long enough to see the tigers and the lion. If it hadn't been for that *nit*, that *nut-case*, that silly *goop*. . . . Under his breath, Sam called Percy all these names and a few others, less polite. Then, feeling a little better, he went up to the big van that had been drawn up close to the tent, to see if he could hear the old lion moving about.

He was standing with his ear pressed to the cold side of the van when Percy said, behind him, 'Hello, Sam.'

'What *d'you* want?'

'I got out the way you did. I want to play with you,' Percy said simply.

Sam sighed. 'Oh Lord – don't you want to watch the circus?'

'I've been to better circuses than this one. I went to Bertram Mills last Christmas and it was a lot better. So I'd rather play with you now.'

'Well you can't,' Sam said. 'I've got to go and see a friend of mine.'

He shouldn't really have lingered, he thought with a stab of conscience. It was quite dark now, though the moon would be up later, and Abe would be waiting. He remembered suddenly what Abe was waiting *for* – and caught his breath.

'If you don't want to go back to the circus, you'd best run along home, Percy Mountjoy,' he said, and, turning, walked fast across the field, away from the tent.

Percy ran after him. 'Please, Sam.' he trotted beside him, his small face pale in the gloom. 'You can have my stamp collection if you like.'

'I'm not interested in stamps,' Sam said.

'Neither am I. But my mother says it's ever such a nice hobby – wouldn't you like a nice hobby, Sam?'

'No, I wouldn't. Go home.'

'Well, you can have my marbles then. I've got one marble that's ever so big. It's the biggest marble in the whole world.'

'GO HOME.'

'Where you going, Sam?'

There was nothing for it but to out-run him. They had reached the road now. Sam put his head down and sprinted across it; crashed through the hedge at the side of the stone bridge; skidded on the muddy bank of the river and fell flat on his face. He felt a sharp pain just below his eye and knew he had landed on a stone. He sat up and put his hand to his cheek; it felt wet and sticky. Was it blood or mud? He wondered if he should wash it in the river but there was no time because Percy's voice was calling him from the bridge. With a little moan, Sam got to his feet and ran up the field away from the river and the road, up the side of the

Bent Hill. He kept going, up and up, blundering through thorn hedges and marshy patches, until he was winded. Then he stopped and looked back. He could see little in the darkness but the dark shadow of the hedge he had just forced his way through and could hear nothing except his own laboured panting. He wasn't quite sure where he was, but he reckoned that he had climbed a good long way, almost up to the edge of Gibbet Wood. He stood still for a little, trying to get his bearings and finally decided that he had come much higher up the Bent Hill than he had needed to: he was on the edge of the field they had begun ploughing last week and the cob-nut field was some way below him, to the left.

He walked slowly downwards, his legs feeling soft and rubbery beneath him and each breath stabbing like a knife in his ribs. His cut cheek was swollen and throbbing and jarred horribly whenever he stumbled on the freshly ploughed ridges. Since there was no one to hear, he began to whimper a little.

He came to a sparse hedge reinforced with barbed wire, with a ditch on the other side. He felt for the wire and pushed it down with his foot. Then, clinging to a thorn branch, he hoisted himself up and stood, peering down into the cob-nut field with relief. He was tired and sore but he had shaken Percy off, and now, in a minute, he would find Abe, and then he could go home. Home suddenly seemed very attractive. He pursed his lips to whistle for Abe, but before he could make a sound a voice spoke below him, in the ditch.

'Hallo, Sam,' it said.

CHAPTER ELEVEN

IT was Percy. 'Hallo Sam,' he said, for the second time.

Sam gasped and slipped down into the ditch, ripping his jersey on the barbed wire.

'I watched you go up,' Percy said. 'And I guessed this is where you were going 'cause I've watched you go up here before. So I cut across this field and got here before you. Why did you go such a long way round, Sam?'

Sam could not answer for a minute. When his breath came back, he said, 'You couldn't have seen me. *In the dark.*'

'You've got a white shirt on under your jersey,' Percy said. 'And a lot of it's hanging out at the back. *And* I've got very good night vision. My mother says so. She says it's because I eat such a lot of raw carrots. What are we going to do now, Sam?'

'Be quiet for a minute,' Sam said. He got out of the ditch and stood, straining his eyes and listening. Abe had said he might bring Whitey. Was that the white horse over there – that glimmer in the middle of the field?

He slid back down into the ditch beside Percy. 'Listen,' he whispered urgently. 'You go home. I'm telling you for your own good. It's not safe up here.'

'I'm not frightened, Sam,' Percy said. 'Not with you.'

'Don't talk so *loud*. You ought to be frightened. I couldn't save you. Not if . . .' Sam broke off and tried again. 'You just don't *understand*. There's all sorts of wicked people about – robbers and murderers and – and – *kidnap-*

pers. Tell you what, if you go home I'll play with you to-morrow ...'

'I want to play now,' Percy said loudly. 'And I'd love to see a murderer or a kidnapper. I'd specially like to see a kidnapper.'

A faint call came across the field. 'Mas ... Mas ...'

Sam sighed. It was too late. 'All right,' he said grimly, 'don't say you didn't ask for it.' He sighed again and whistled, a gentle, warbling note.

Within seconds there was the thud of hooves and Abe appeared, on Whitey.

'*Oh,*' Percy said on a high, treble note. '*Oh* ...' He moved close to Sam and seized hold of his jersey.

'Don't be scared,' Abe said gently. He slid off the mare's back. 'You han't scared him, Sam?'

'No,' Sam said in a dull voice. He knew that he hadn't the courage not to go through with it now. Abe would think his such a coward. Oh – if only Percy hadn't followed him. If only *he* hadn't pushed his way under the tent and given Percy a chance to follow him! 'We're playing kidnappers,' Sam said. 'That what you want, Percy?'

'That would be *lovely,*' Percy said.

Abe and Sam grinned at each other sheepishly. Neither of them knew what to do next.

'Come *on,*' Percy said. 'We'll play that you kidnap me now and hide me somewhere. Where'll you hide me, Sam?'

Abe said awkwardly, 'We couldn't tell you that. T'wouldn't be safe, see?'

Percy nodded solemnly. 'When I escaped, I'd be able to lead the police straight to your hide-out. Well – you'd better blindfold me, hadn't you? Then I shan't know where you're taking me.'

He smiled happily at Abe and Sam. They didn't move. Mention of the police had rooted them to the ground.

'G-go on,' Percy urged them. 'Haven't you got a hanky or something?'

Sam stared at him as if hypnotized. His hand crept slowly to his pocket. 'Mine isn't very clean,' he said.

'You can have mine, then,' Percy said. 'I've got two. One for blow and one for show. You can have the clean one.' He whipped a folded handkerchief out of his shirt pocket and handed it to Sam. Then he turned round meekly and waited.

Sam folded the handkerchief and placed it over Percy's eyes. His fingers were trembling so badly that he couldn't tie the knot. 'I can't *see*,' he said crossly.

'Wait on a minute, I got a torch,' Abe said. He tugged at his pocket and then shone a bright beam on to Sam's face. 'Why, you're all over blood, Sam,' he said in a horrified voice.

'S'nothing, I just got cut a bit. Shine it on the knot, though, you're dazzling my eyes.'

Percy said, 'I expect you cut yourself when you fell down running away from me.'

'I wasn't. . . .' Sam drew a deep breath and decided to say no more. He glanced sidelong at Abe but he was gazing at the back of Percy's head and didn't appear to have noticed anything. 'You're making a fair old mess of that knot,' was all he said.

'You do it, then.'

Sam held the torch while Abe tied the handkerchief.

Percy fidgeted. 'Bit tighter,' he ordered. 'I can see through the bottom. That's better. Now turn me round three times.'

'We're not playing Blind Man's Buff,' Sam said coldly. He examined Abe's torch. It shone red and green as well as white like the torches Mr Ivor Davies had in his hardware store – Sam had noticed them last Saturday morning when he had gone there to buy a new kettle for his mother. 'It's smashing,' he said enviously, 'Did you get it from Ivor Davies's?'

'No,' Abe said, and Sam knew at once that it had been a silly question: where would Abe have got the money to buy a torch like this?

'Where'd you get it then?' he asked.

There was a short silence. 'Oh – I jus' found it,' Abe muttered.

'*Found* it?'

'Jus' – jus' lying about.' Abe sounded strangely uncomfortable. 'I found it in Gibbet Wood.'

'In the *wood*?' Sam said incredulously. He twirled the torch in his hand and switched the coloured lights on and off. It was a beautiful torch, shiny and almost new, the batteries were powerful: it was not the sort of torch you were likely to find lying in the damp undergrowth of Gibbet Wood. A miserable suspicion crept into Sam's mind and although he only said, 'That's funny – I mean it's not rusty or anything,' Abe must have guessed what he was thinking because he snatched the torch roughly out of Sam's hand and switched it off.

'I didn't steal it, anyways,' he said angrily.

Sam blinked. The red and green lights were still flashing in front of his eyes. 'I didn't mean ...' he began, and then stopped guiltily: it was just what he had meant – or half meant, anyway ...

'What did you mean then?' Abe said. The moon had half risen now and Sam could see his face, set and pale.

'Dono really. I just thought ...'

'You jus' thought *what*?' Abe advanced on Sam, fists clenched, eyes glinting dangerously.

Sam thought quickly. It seemed odd to him that Abe should mind so much being accused of stealing – *he* wouldn't have minded, he thought – but he was in no mood for a fight; he was tired and his cut cheek was sore and aching. 'Nothing really,' he said, 'I just thought you might have borrowed some money from your Gran, you said she kept some under her mattress.'

'D'you think I'd tek her money?' Abe said contemptuously. And then he gasped and flung himself at Sam who went down flat on his back. The pain in his cheek leapt up sharply as he hit his head on the ground and he gave a little cry; perhaps it was because of this that Abe had not hit him, but merely sat on his stomach and said, 'You're a rotten louse, Sam Peach, I found that torch and I was goin' to tell you 'bout it, but I won't now, not ever, I won't *ever* tell you, not *ever* . . .'

'STOP FIGHTING,' Percy shouted suddenly. His high clear voice rang out like a sudden bell. Abe fell silent. He got slowly off Sam and Sam stood up. They both looked at Percy who stood with his head on one side and said plaintively. 'I'm getting bored just standing here listening to you fighting. Aren't we going to get on with the game?'

Neither Sam nor Abe answered him. They glanced uncomfortably at each other.

'Well,' Percy said. 'Aren't you going to take me to your hide-out?'

Silence.

'Is it far?' Percy said.

Abe cleared his throat. 'It's quite a way.'

'Then I'd better ride on the horse, hadn't I?' Percy said. He wriggled with excitement. 'Oh, *please*. I've always wanted to ride on a horse.'

The old mare was cropping the grass. Very slowly, Abe went up to her, took her bridle and led her over to Percy.

'Hurry *up*,' Percy said. 'I can't get on the horse by myself, can I?'

Abe looked helplessly at Sam. Helplessly, as if they were both caught up in a dream, the two boys hoisted Percy up on to the old mare's hollow back. 'Give me the reins,' Percy ordered. Abe put the reins in his hands.

'Giddup,' Percy shouted exultantly, and beat his small heels against old Whitey's fat paunch.

She blew out through her nose and shuddered all along her back, making Percy squeal with excitement.

Abe took hold of her bridle, steadying her, and stared at Sam through his long fringe of hair. 'You'd best git home 'fore he's missed,' he said stiffly.

Sam had the feeling that Abe was suddenly unwilling to go on with the kidnapping as he had been earlier, but, because they had quarrelled, he did not know how to admit it. Sam did not know what to say either, so he said nothing.

Abe tossed the hair back from his eyes and Sam could see his throat moving as he swallowed hard. He said softly. 'I won't scare him, I'll go on letting him think it's jus' a game, so he won't be scared.'

'What are you whispering about?' Percy asked crossly. 'I can't hear properly with this hanky over my eyes.'

'Nothing,' Sam said.

He stood back and watched them go. Abe looked back once or twice but Sam couldn't see the expression on his face. When they were out of sight, he turned and blundered homewards. His head hurt as if a little man with a hammer was banging about inside it, and his heart felt like a lump of lead.

Abe and Percy – kidnapper and kidnapped – were silent for a while. Leading Whitey carefully, so that the old horse shouldn't stumble, Abe wondered what Percy was feeling, sitting blindfold on her back. He hadn't seemed frightened to begin with and he didn't look frightened now but what people felt didn't always show in their faces. And he was a very little boy . . .

Abe said, 'Dessay you could do with a bite of supper, couldn't you? Tell you what, we'll have a bit of something just as soon as we git to – well, just as soon as we git to where we're goin'. You c'n have just about what you like – there's lots of chocolate an' stuff, and then you c'n git straight to bed . . .'

'I don't want to go to bed,' Percy said in a high, whining voice.

'Well, you needn't then.' Abe said quickly. 'Not straight-away, I mean – there's all sorts of things we c'n do.'

'What things?'

'Well . . .' Abe considered. 'We c'n go out in the woods a bit. We c'n go and look at my traps. I set some rabbit traps with a bit of wire, t'other day.'

'I've never been allowed out at night before,' Percy said. 'My mother says the night air's bad for my chest. She's afraid I'll catch pneumonia. She's always afraid I'll catch something and die.'

Abe looked up at him. Percy looked very small and frail and young, suddenly; the bandage round his eyes made his head look heavy – too heavy for his frail neck which seemed to droop sideways like a flower stalk.

'You're not sick now, are you?' he asked uneasily.

'I don't *think* I am,' Percy sighed. 'But sometimes she says I'm ill when I don't feel ill, so I can't tell, can I?'

His mouth turned down as if he were going to cry. Of course he *must* be frightened, Abe thought – frightened stiff and missing his mother.

He said gently, 'S'all right, Perce. Don't cry. I'm not goin' to hurt you or anythin' and I'll git that ole band-age off your eyes in a minute. So you've no call to be scared . . .'

'*Scared?*' Percy said. His voice was squeaky with astonishment. '*Scared?*' He sat bolt upright on Whitey's back. 'I'm not scared,' he said. 'This is the best game I've ever been in, in my whole life.'

CHAPTER TWELVE

'That's a nasty cut,' Mr Peach said. 'Where did you get it?'

'I fell on a stone,' Sam said. He looked down at his muddied shorts and his torn jersey and then glanced nervously at his father. But Mr Peach did not comment on his appearance. He sat Sam down by the fire, went to fetch water and towels and began, very gently, to bathe Sam's cheek. It seemed to take a long time and hurt a great deal. Sam doubled his fists in his lap and stared hard at his father's waistcoat buttons.

'Nearly done,' Mr Peach said. 'Your mother won't be long. She's gone to fetch Rose from the circus. Do you feel all right?'

Sam nodded, though in fact he felt curiously cold and sweaty and, when he tried to look up, his father's long, anxious face seemed to quiver suddenly like a reflection in water.

Mr Peach's voice came from a long way away. 'Put your head between your knees.' Sam felt his father's hand on the back of his neck, pressing him forward and down. There was a strange, sea-like booming in his ears. He felt as if he were being drawn into a long, dark tunnel . . .

Then he was sitting up again. Water was trickling down the back of his neck and his father was kneeling in front of him, a soaking flannel in his hand.

'I felt funny,' Sam said weakly.

'You fainted.' His father's face was worried. 'I can't think where your mother has got to,' he grumbled, and then went to fetch a glass of water which he made Sam sip, very slowly.

As he felt better, Sam began to be very proud of his achievement. 'I fainted,' he informed his mother and Rose when they came in. 'Didn't I Dad? I fainted dead away.'

To his annoyance, they did not seem as impressed as he had expected them to be. Rose barely glanced at him and, though Mrs Peach said, 'Oh, poor Sam,' and stroked his forehead, it was in an abstracted way as if she had more important things to think about.

'Wherever did you get to?' Mr Peach asked her in an accusing tone. 'I thought you were never coming.'

'I'm sorry, dear. But there's been such a fuss – you can't imagine!' She pulled off her headscarf and patted her hair. 'Mrs Mountjoy's lost her Percy. She was waiting for him outside the tent when I got there and he didn't come out with the others – oh, you never heard such a hullabaloo!'

Rose did look at Sam now. Her cheeks were puffed out tight, like small balloons. Forgetting he was an invalid, Sam sat bolt upright and, with a cautious eye on his parents, gave Rose a small, telling nod. Rose squeaked, and went red.

'Of course we all helped her look in the tent and the field, but he wasn't there,' Mrs Peach said. 'Mrs Finch has taken her home – she's going to wait with her and make her a cup of tea and try to calm her down.' She smiled, both sympathetic and amused. '*That* won't be easy, I imagine. The poor soul's in such a state!'

'Understandable, don't you think?' Mr Peach said, rather tartly. 'Has anyone told the police?'

Mrs Peach looked astonished. 'Whatever for? Goodness – the boy's only been missing for half an hour. He'll turn up directly, boys always do.'

'I'm glad you're so sure of that, my dear.' Mr Peach was

sarcastic because, to his mind, Mrs Mountjoy's son was not an ordinary boy. Why, Mr Mountjoy was a rich and influential man and his wife had a mink coat and a Jaguar car!

'Of course I'm sure,' Mrs Peach said, bewildered. 'Boys go missing every day. Don't you remember that time Sam disappeared – when he was away all afternoon and most of the evening and I was half out of my mind with worry? You told me not to fuss . . .'

Two red spots appeared on Mr Peach's cheekbones. 'I shall go and see if there is anything I can do,' he said heavily. 'Since Mr Mountjoy is away from home, it is the very least I can do.'

Mrs Peach was surprised to find Rose and Sam so willing to go to bed. She had expected they would try to stay up as long as they could in order to hear what had happened to Percy. But they talked about other things while they ate their supper and showed no interest in the missing boy, even when Mrs Peach promised that as soon as Sam's father came home, she would run upstairs and let them know if Percy had been found.

'Oh, I shouldn't bother, Auntie, I expect we'll be fast asleep,' Rose said, and gave an artificial little yawn.

'I won't think of disturbing you, then,' Mrs Peach said.

She looked rather shocked.

There was no question of sleep, of course. They sat up in Rose's bed, whispering. 'Was it awfully difficult?' Rose wanted to know.

'Well – we had a bit of a fight once he knew what I was going to do with him,' Sam said. 'I beat him in the end but t'wasn't easy – he's quite strong, for all he's so little, an' he was pretty desperate of course, an' when people are desperate they have ten times their ordinary strength.'

There was a little silence. Then Rose said, 'You didn't hurt him, did you, Sam?'

'*I* was the one that got hurt,' Sam said in an injured tone.

'I know. Poor Sam. But Percy – he wasn't *too* frightened, was he?'

Sam hesitated. 'Well, no. Well – no, I wouldn't say he was frightened, exactly ...'

It seemed a long time before Mr Peach came home. Rose was almost asleep when Sam heard his father's key in the front door and his step in the hall.

He heard something else, too : a low, muffled sobbing.

Sam nudged Rose awake : they slid out of bed and crept to the top of the stairs. Mr Peach was alone in the hall; the bald patch on the top of his head glistened under the hall light. The sitting-room door was open; the sobbing came from inside the room. They heard Mrs Peach's voice, '... oh, my poor dear ... sit yourself down and rest a minute ...'

Then she came into the hall and shut the door. Mr Peach spoke to her in a low voice. Hardly daring to breathe, the listeners on the landing heard that Percy had not come home; the police had been informed and Sergeant Smeath had gone out with a band of volunteers to search for him. Various children had been roused from their sleep and questioned but none of them remembered seeing Percy at the circus; it was now conjectured that he had left the tent before the performance was over, wandered off on his own and got lost in the darkness. Mr Peach said he was sure no harm had come to him, but he had been unable to persuade Mrs Mountjoy to take this optimistic view. She was so distracted with grief that Doctor Davis had been summoned; he had prescribed a sleeping pill and suggested that she should spend the night with a neighbour – it would be bad for her to sit up in her own house, waiting and worrying.

Mrs Finch had offered to stay in the Mountjoy house in case Percy returned and Mr Peach had brought his mother home with him. . . . 'Naturally, I will join the search party,' Mr Peach said gallantly.

'Of course I'll look after her, the poor soul,' Mrs Peach said. Then she paused a minute before adding, softly, 'Though if it was my Sam, I know what *I'd* be doing! I'd be out looking for him!'

'Mrs Mountjoy is a very sensitive woman,' Mr Peach said in a grave, reproachful voice.

Mrs Peach gave a little sigh and said that if he was going tramping about the fields, Mr Peach had better take the big flash lamp and wear his rubber boots.

After her husband had gone, she stood for a moment alone in the hall, her head bowed, her shoulders drooping. Then she straightened her back and seemed to brace herself. She opened the sitting-room door.

Rose and Sam heard her muffled voice, talking soothingly to Mrs Mountjoy and then a wild outburst of weeping that made them glance at each other and move closer, for comfort.

'. . . a nice glass of warm milk and a hot water bottle,' Mrs Peach said, and then, 'Now, now, don't upset yourself so, of course we'll talk instead if you'd rather . . . Let's try and think, perhaps we can think of something useful. Has Percy any friends he might have gone off with . . . just for a joke, of course . . . you know what boys are . . .'

Mrs Mountjoy did her best to answer. Her words floated up to the listeners on the stairs, between ejaculations of grief. '. . . no friends . . . poor little Percy . . . all my own fault . . . all the boys here so rough . . . I wouldn't let him . . .' There followed a spate of sobs that made most of her words unintelligible and then a coherent sentence 'Oh, I've been such a bad mother, I see it now; he said only the other day "Oh

Mummy I'm so lonely, I've got no one to play with, couldn't we ask Sam to tea?", and I said no, I'd seen Sam with such a dreadful, low-down, common boy that I couldn't believe he was the right playmate for my little Percy, and he gave me such a sad look – I shall never forget it till my dying day – and went off to watch the boys on the green, just sitting there on the bench and not joining in! Oh, it breaks my heart now to think of it!'

Mrs Peach said in a restrained voice that perhaps Mrs Mountjoy had been wrong in not allowing Percy to play with the village boys, but there was no point in upsetting herself now.

But Mrs Mountjoy could not be consoled. She continued to accuse herself: she had been a wicked, unkind woman, depriving Percy of the companionship he longed for, and now she had been punished for it – she had lost him, he was lying dead somewhere! At the very least he was badly injured, lying somewhere alone in the dark and the cold. 'Oh, my Percy, my little Percy,' she cried, 'what can have happened to him?' A fresh fear arrived to torment her. 'Suppose he has been kidnapped?' she sobbed.

'Gracious Heaven! Who would kidnap a boy in Castle Stoke?' Mrs Peach said robustly, and then, in an altered tone, 'Oh don't – please don't cry so. I shall cry myself in a minute. I know how I should feel if it were my Sam.' Her own voice wavered and then all the children could hear was the quiet sobbing of the two women.

Feeling guilty, Rose and Sam crept away from the head of the stairs. At Rose's door, they looked at each other.

'I reckon we'll have to send him back tomorrow,' Sam said.

'What'll Abe say?'

Sam shrugged. 'Whatever he says, we can't go on with it, that's all. I mean we just can't, can we?'

Rose sighed regretfully. 'No, I suppose we can't '

They parted with subdued good nights. Sam climbed into bed and yawned. Within a few minutes he heard the pad of bare feet and Rose was standing by his bed, ghostly in her white nightdress. 'Sam,' she whispered. 'I've just thought of something awful. If we send Percy back, he'll tell on us, won't he?'

Sam's pulse leapt in his throat. He had always known there was something wrong with their plan: this was it! 'I suppose he will,' he said slowly.

Rose swallowed. 'What do they do to kidnappers, Sam?'

'Prison,' Sam said in a hollow voice. 'They get sent to prison.'

Rose began to shake. She climbed into bed beside Sam and lay, quivering with silent sobs. For a little while Sam was too taken up with the dreadful prospect before them to comfort her but then, slowly, his courage returned. He put his arm round Rose. 'It's all right,' he said. 'They can't do anything to you – only to Abe and me. You weren't there, so Percy can't tell on you, can he? And *I* won't tell – nor'll Abe, you can count on that.'

'Oh Sam, you are *nice*.' Rose drew a long, shuddering breath, and then began to cry again.

Sam held her tight. 'Don't cry. We'll say it was just our plan, Abe's and mine. We won't tell on you, whatever they do.'

Uplifted by this noble promise, he began to feel calm and peaceful. He had always wanted to do something heroic – now was his chance!

'We won't tell, even if they torture us,' he said.

CHAPTER THIRTEEN

When Sam and Rose left for school the next morning, Mrs Mountjoy was still sleeping. So was Mr Peach, who had returned from his fruitless search in the small hours. Mrs Peach looked white and tired as she gave the children their breakfast and told them Percy was still missing. 'What I'm going to say to that poor woman when she wakes up, I can't think!' she mourned.

At the end of the first lesson, Sam told Miss Pennyfather that he felt sick. He clutched at his stomach and rolled his eyes in such a realistic way that she believed him and sent him home.

Once outside the playground, he made as fast as he could to Abe's shack. The door stood open; after calling Abe and getting no answer, Sam went in to find the place empty. The shack was dark; the only window was small and covered by a thick, dusty curtain; a heavily carved, oak dresser that would have looked large in an empty cathedral, took up the whole of one wall and dwarfed the room. The only other furniture was a wooden table and chair, a sagging brass bed and an old-fashioned horse-hair sofa with rolled wooden ends. Some rough blankets were neatly folded upon it. A sleepy wood fire whispered in the grate: there was no other sound.

Though Sam was glad to have this chance of seeing inside Mrs Tanner's shack, the quiet made him nervous: he kept glancing over his shoulder as if afraid she might suddenly materialize in one of the corners. He began to feel chilled in spite of the fire, and went outside where a pale, drained-looking sun was beginning to lift over the white, morning mist.

'Abe,' Sam called, and his voice echoed in the hollow.

The old mare lifted her head and looked at him. She was tethered to an iron bar driven into the ground.

'Abe,' Sam shouted again, and, below him, a pigeon flapped away from a tree in Gibbet Wood.

Sam climbed to the top of the bluff and looked down at the valleys on either side. A toy tractor was ploughing one of the coloured fields, gulls wheeling in its wake; toy cars buzzed along the thread-like roads; on the far hill, sheep ran like a flock of insects, a dark speck yapping at their heels.

Sam sat on his haunches and wondered why things looked small when they were a long way away.

Abe and Percy did not appear for a long time. Sam had given up shouting; he had even given up looking for them and was simply enjoying his idle morning, lying on his back and trying to stare straight into the watery sun, when they emerged from Gibbet Wood and began to climb up to the old mine. They advanced softly on the sheep-cropped turf and the first thing Sam knew of their approach was hearing Percy's high-pitched giggle.

'You didn't see us, Sam, we crept up on you like spies,' Percy said triumphantly.

He looked quite different from Mrs Mountjoy's treasured little son. His face was filthy and his uncombed, yellow hair stuck up in spikes making him look like a dirty, wet canary. He was wearing Sam's old football jersey which had been none too clean to start with and now was less so: it hung down almost to his knees, after passing over a mysterious bulge in the region of his stomach.

'Oh *Sam*,' he cried, 'I'm having a lovely time.'

'We bin collecting mushrooms,' Abe said shortly. 'Mushrooms an' sherbet dabs, that's what he fancies for dinner!'

Percy's face glowed. 'I'll start on peeling the mushrooms, shall I, Abe? You said I could.'

Abe nodded. Looking harassed, he began to unfasten a knife from his belt. It was a very new-looking knife.

'Where'd you get that?' Sam asked.

Abe looked at him warily. 'Same place I got the torch.'

Sam felt himself go red. 'Where's that? Go on, Abe – tell me where you got them.'

Abe shook his head. 'No. I won't tell you. I said I wouldn't, yesterday.'

He turned his back on Sam and tossed the knife to Percy who cut his finger trying to open it. He bawled like a stuck pig, but only for a minute while Sam tied up the bleeding finger with his dirty handkerchief; then he stopped crying and gave a tug at his jersey, releasing all the big, field mushrooms that had been hidden there. He settled down on the ground with a little sigh of pleasure, and began to peel off their tough, outer skins.

The other two walked out of earshot. Sam longed to know where Abe had got the knife and the torch but did not dare ask again. Instead, he explained about Mrs Mountjoy and how he and Rose had decided Percy must go home. 'It was awful, she was crying and moaning,' he said, looking uneasily at Abe and wondering how he would take this betrayal of their plan, but Abe just shrugged his shoulders and said, 'S'all right by me. I'm not too stuck on the idea now, I c'n tell you.' He kicked moodily at a stone and then burst out, 'I've had enough, I tell you. I'm not a ruddy nurse maid. D'you know, he can't even dress himself – his Mam's always done it, he says. An' that's not the worst of it. I got to play with him all the time – all last night he kep' saying what fun it was, sleeping in this funny little house, an' he wouldn't go to sleep, nor let me, neither! D'you know what I done most of last night?' Abe's voice rose. Sam shook his head. 'I sat up in bed an' I played "I Spy".'

'I expect he was over-excited,' Sam said tolerantly.

Abe's face contorted with disgust. 'He don't *act* right. He oughter be scared and beggin' for mercy, but he ain't. Not a bit of it. He acts jus' as if he was on holiday—as if this was jus' something we arranged for *fun*. Well, I tell you straight, Sam, I don't mind being a robber or something an' getting some money so Rose c'n fly off to America, but I ain't running no holiday home for kids, not for a million pounds!' He held his hand out straight in front of him. It quivered slightly. 'Look at that!' he cried with a fresh spasm of indignation. 'My nerves is all shot to pieces after jus' one night!'

'It might've been better to have kidnapped a grown person,' Sam admitted. But there were more important things to discuss at this moment than what they might have done. 'What's he going to tell Mrs Mountjoy when he gets back? He'll tell her it was you and me took him off and then we'll be in dead trouble. Prison, I should think.' He sighed: the prospect seemed a good deal less heroic than it had done last night.

'Kids don't get sent to prison, they get sent to reformatory,' Abe said scornfully. 'Didn't you know that?' He paused. 'We'll jus' have to make him promise not to tell. We'll tell him t'aint jus' a game, that we're real kidnappers – a real gang. Then I reckon he'll promise all right. I mean he'll be so glad not to be kidnapped any more that I 'spect he'll promise anything, jus' about.'

But it didn't work out like that. Percy seemed unimpressed when they told him this was not just a game. And when they broke the joyful news that he was to be returned to his home and his mother forthwith, he burst into tears.

'I wanna stay here,' he wailed. 'I like being kidnapped. I'm having a lovely time and I don't *want* to go home.'

Sam thought fast. 'You'll get awful hungry if you don't,' he warned him. 'I mean, there's not much for dinner today, is there? And there'll be less tomorrow.' His own stomach was beginning to feel empty, so he was able to put considerable force into this argument. 'Wouldn't you like a proper dinner now – meat and gravy and greens and potatoes? And – and perhaps ice-cream afterwards?'

Percy shook his head. 'The food's nicer here than at home. I've had lots and lots of chocolate and I'm not allowed sweets at home because of my teeth.'

Sam tried another tack. 'Your Mum's awfully upset. She misses you dreadfully. She cried and cried last night.'

'Did she cry much?' Percy asked in an interested voice.

'Buckets and buckets. And if you don't go home, she'll just go on crying – you don't want to upset her like that, do you?'

Percy did not answer, but a little smile began at his mouth and spread wider and wider until his whole face was one huge, happy grin.

Sam was shocked at this callousness. He said in a cross voice, 'Well, it doesn't matter what you *want* – you got to go home.'

'Won't go,' Percy said.

'You'll do as you're told.'

'I won't. Won't, won't, *won't*.' Percy stuck his legs out in front of him and drummed his heels on the ground.

'You *will*. We'll *make* you.'

Percy's heels stopped drumming. He looked at Sam with an evil grin in his eye.

'If you make me go home,' he said, 'I'll tell my mother you tied me up and starved me and ... and ... *tortured* me. Chinese burns and things like that. Then you'll get into dreadful trouble.'

Abe and Sam stared at him, their mouths open. It was unbelievable that a little boy of seven could be capable of such wickedness. Unbelievable, but true: they looked at his bland, fishy gaze and knew that Percy was capable of anything.

He smiled triumphantly. 'Tell you what,' he said. 'I'll go home tomorrow. *If*,' – his blue eyes swept from Sam to Abe – '*if* Abe'll take me into Gibbet Wood tonight and show me the Gibbet and the Headless Hunter. I've never seen a Gibbet or a ghost,' he added, rather pathetically.

'You'd be scared to death,' Sam said.

'I wouldn't,' Percy's expression was contemptuous. 'I'm never scared of anything.'

Sam opened his mouth to make one last protest but Abe said, suddenly and unexpectedly, 'All right, then.'

'I thought you'd be sensible,' Percy said in a horribly adult way. 'Now we're going to build a fire and cook the mushrooms, aren't we?'

In silence, the two bigger boys collected dry planks for a fire which they built in a hollow between two rocks. It was soon blazing merrily, cooking the mushrooms in an iron pan and Sam was growing very conscious of the aching, empty space beneath his ribs. He looked at Percy's gold wrist watch and saw that it was already half past two.

They ate the mushrooms with stale sliced bread, and finished off the meal with sherbet dabs. Sam and Abe had one each; Percy two.

'I want to go and look for puff-balls now,' he said, when he had finished.

Sam was glad to move because, although the sun shone thinly, the air was cold. In the shadow of Gibbet Wood the frost still lingered hairily on the grass and the leaves were brittle beneath their feet. There were no puff-balls on the edge of the wood and Abe and Sam watched gloomily while Percy climbed trees, shrieking with excitement and showering them with twigs and yellow leaves.

'You'd think he'd never climbed a tree before,' Sam said disgustedly.

'Far as I c'n gather, his Mam's never let him.'

Sam sighed. 'He's got to go home tonight, Abe, he's just *got* to.'

'You go home, bit later on, an' I'll see what I c'n do,' Abe said 'He'll heed me better when you're not there. I c'n promise him something – like coming up one night to see the Hunter. T'wouldn't be any good tonight, see, 'cause there's goin' to be a clear sky.' He sniffed at the sharpening air. 'Fine clear sky and a good moon, I'd say.'

And there Sam had to leave it, though his conscience went on troubling him about poor Mrs Mountjoy, all the time they were looking for puff-balls. They found great clumps a little further into the wood: big, round, purple-patched beauties that exploded fine black dust when they stamped on them. Percy stamped and stamped and the dust flew round him; it got in his yellow hair and clung to the sticky sherbet that had dried round his mouth. He looked like a chimney sweep.

'Mind you don't swallow any, that stuff's poison,' Abe warned him.

'Oh, don't *fuss*,' Percy said. 'Come on, now, let's go to the gibbet. I want to see all the dead animals. I *like* dead animals.'

Abe looked thoughtful. 'I'm not sure as I ought to. I mean I'm not sure I ought to tek you there.'

'But you *said* you would,' Percy shrieked.

'I know, but I bin thinking, since.' Abe sat down on an old tree stump and began prodding at an ant heap with a stick. '*First*,' he said slowly, 'there's a secret about the gibbet that I'm not sure I ought to let anyone else know. Even Sam doesn't know. An' *second,* it's a pretty wild old place. Even Sam's scared to go there, ain't you, Sam?'

He looked up at Sam through his tangled hair, his eyes bright and compelling. 'Go on, Sam, tell him you're scared,' he said.

Sam saw that Abe was trying to make the gibbet extra attractive to Percy, but all the same it went against the grain to admit he was afraid. He hesitated, wondering if there really was a secret about the gibbet or if Abe was just pretending. He sighed. 'Well, I am just a bit scared,' he admitted unwillingly.

Abe looked at Percy. 'You see? I mean you'd jus' go back an' tell your Mam an' – well – she'll be mad enough as it is, but if she finds out I took you to the gibbet, she'll fair do for me.' He heaved a long sigh, gave the ant heap a final swish with his stick and stood up. 'No – I jus' can't risk it, Percy.'

Percy's eyes were snapping with excitement. 'Oh – please, Abe. Please – I won't tell. I won't tell anything, not about you kidnapping me or *anything*. I'll just say I got lost and . . . and . . . slept up in the woods or something. Oh Abe – if you take me to the gibbet, I'll do anything you say?'

'Sure? *Will you go home this evening?*'

Percy hesitated. He looked from one boy to the other.

'There really is a secret about the gibbet, Abe?'

Abe nodded.

'And you don't know what it is, Sam?'

'No, I don't.'

Percy smiled to himself. 'And are you *really* scared of the gibbet?'

Sam nodded slowly.

'Honest? Cross your heart?'

'Cross my heart and hope to die,' Sam said, and felt himself begin to blush.

'You won't come with us then?'

'No. I'm going home.'

Percy jumped up and down on the puff-balls while the black dust flew. 'Sam's scared, Sam's scared,' he chanted. '*I'm* not scared, Abe.'

'You won't go, though, les' you promise,' Abe said. He nodded good-bye to Sam in a friendly way and jerked his thumb up, as a sign of triumph. But Sam did not reply. His ears burned as he stumbled away through the undergrowth and heard Percy's high, excited voice. 'You and me's not scared of the old gibbet, are we, Abe? Not like silly old Sam?'

The taunt rang in Sam's mind long after he was out of earshot and skirting the lower edge of the wood on his way home. He realized that the gibbet would not have been nearly so effective a bargaining counter with Percy if he, Sam, had not admitted to being afraid of it – all the same, the shame burned deep into his soul. He had told a seven year old that he was afraid! Oh – how horrible! He would never live it down – never!

When he reached the cob-nut tree, shame and misery overcame him altogether and he flung himself down on his stomach and moaned aloud, burying his hot face in the dampening grass. He didn't want to go home, he didn't want to *live*.

When his despair had abated a little, he sat up, leaning against the tree trunk and whistling loudly to show the world – and himself – that he didn't care. Why should he care that a silly baby of seven thought he was a coward? *He* knew he wasn't. Hadn't he, only the other day, fought Stan Meath, the biggest bully in the school? He had lost ignominiously and had his nose rubbed in the mud but at least he had stood his ground where most boys would have run. He had climbed the rotten elm tree in the churchyard; he had sailed a raft down over the dreadful 'rapids' of the Castle River; he had endured five fillings in his back teeth without uttering a single cry; he had stolen apples from old Miss Bason's orchard – which was more than most boys dared to do, Miss Bason being agile for her age and handy with a stick.

Listing these brave deeds encouraged Sam. He decided to add to them in order to recover his pride completely. Before he went home he would go into the field that had the bull in it – not any bull, *the* bull: Farmer Rogers' prize bull that was noted for its evil temper.

The field lay some way off and it was growing dark when Sam got there. He frowned at the notice, *Beware of the Bull,* and, climbing the gate, sat poised on the top bar, looking for the menacing shadow in the dusk. But the field was empty. Sam stood precariously on the top of the gate and looked round. Not only was this field empty, but the next one which usually contained Farmer Rogers' prize Guernsey herd, was empty too. This puzzled Sam – surely it was past milking time? He shook his head, sighed, and climbed down.

He wandered along the road, kicking at the loose chippings, on the alert for some other feat of agility or daring. Nothing came to his mind except tree-climbing, and he passed an alarming half hour climbing an oak tree. It was now almost completely dark and the exercise was both difficult and dangerous but it was not until he had missed his footing on one of the high, gnarled branches and saved himself by a hair's breadth from crashing to the ground, that Sam felt his honour was sufficiently satisfied to allow him to go home.

Percy, though Sam didn't know it, had gone home before him.

He had spent a very happy hour at the gibbet: the dangling, dead animals had reminded him of his mother.

'*She's* got a fox's fur,' he explained to Abe, 'and the fox's head is still hanging on it. So she's like a sort of gibbet herself, isn't she?' He giggled wildly and Abe was rather shocked.

'I think you'd best git home now,' he said.

'Not yet.' Percy looked at him cunningly. 'There's one more thing you promised. You haven't told me the secret yet,' he said.

Curiously, Abe looked shy. 'Well – t'aint much, really,' he said slowly. 'It's jus' about the hollow inside the ole tree. Sometimes – sometimes there's things inside.'

'Treasure?' Percy asked, eyes wide.

'Well – sort of.' Abe paused, and then went on reluctantly, 'You know my knife? Well – I found that there, t'other day – most times I come, I find something in the ole tree. It's only happened jus' lately, an' I jus' find one thing at a time. There was the knife an' the torch, an' one day I found a pair of gum boots. Mine was jus' about worn through an' these fitted. It was jus' like – well, it was jus' like . . .'

'*Magic?*' Percy breathed.

Abe shuffled his feet. 'Well – I dono 'bout that.' His face flamed. 'I dono, but I got the feeling that they was meant for me.'

'Do you mean the fairies put them there?'

'Fairies is rubbish.'

'My mother believes in fairies,' Percy said. 'She's always reading me stories . . .' His eyes danced. 'Oh, Abe, do you think there's anything inside the tree now?'

'You c'n look if you like. 'Long as you promise to git home straight after.'

Percy gave a little sigh. 'All right. I promise.'

Abe hoisted him up. Percy squeaked. 'There's a brown bag!' It was a carrier bag full of apples.

'Magic apples,' Percy cried. 'Can I have one, Abe?'

'You c'n have two. 'Long as you don't eat 'em till you're out of the wood an' on your way – on your way *home*.' He stopped, to let this sink in and looked at Percy gravely. ''Course – you know if they're magic apples, they might do something funny. Make you grow big or something – big as a giant or small as a mouse . . .'

Percy's face glowed. 'Come on, Abe, I'll go home now,' he said.

'You'd best take off Sam's jersey first,' Abe said. 'Otherwise your Mam'll wonder where you got it.'

They stuffed the jersey into the tree trunk. This done, Percy could not get out of the wood fast enough. Abe saw him out of the wood and halfway down the fields, towards the town. It was dusk: they parted at just about the same time that Sam was sitting on the gate, looking for the bull in Farmer Rogers' field.

From the shadow of the hedge, a strange grey shape watched their parting. It lifted its dog-like head – though it was not a dog, nor a fox – and looked curiously after the little boy as he trotted down the field, hopefully munching his first apple. But Percy's way led towards the lights of the town and the creature did not care to follow him there. Instead, after standing quite still for a minute – so still that it seemed no more than a shadow in the shadow of the hedge – it began to move silently and steadily uphill, towards the wood.

It appeared to be following Abe.

CHAPTER FOURTEEN

WHEN Sam got back to Castle Stoke, the moon was just lifting over the church tower. Full, round and clear, it shone down upon a curiously empty street – curiously empty of children, that is: little groups of men stood talking in low voices outside the public houses. They were so absorbed that none of them noticed Sam as he slipped by.

Sam was surprised to see no boys around. Winter or summer, the boys of Castle Stoke stayed out till called indoors at eight or nine o'clock, but tonight, for some strange reason, the town was as empty of young life as if the Pied Piper had just passed through.

It made Sam nervous. He had hoped to arrive back in time to mingle with his friends just as if he had come out of school with them and not bothered to go home for tea. That way, with luck, his mother would never know he had played truant for most of the day.

But it seemed as if his luck was out. He could not even slip quietly inside the house and lie low, because Mrs Peach was waiting for him on the doorstep. As soon as she saw him, she let out a loud cry, 'Oh Sam – thank God,' seized him with both hands and drew him indoors. Once in the hall, she folded him tightly in her arms and began hugging and kissing him.

Since Sam's mother was not the kissing sort, this rapturous reception made him go rigid with astonishment.

At last she gave up hugging him and held him a little away, so she could look into his face. 'Where have you been, you wicked boy?' she asked tenderly, and then, when Sam was too dumb-founded to answer, she began shaking him hard so that his head waggled loosely backwards and forwards like a rag doll's.

'Stop it, Mum,' he protested, half-laughing, half-scared, 'you'll have my head off in a minute.'

She let him go, but said, 'I'll do worse than that, if you don't tell me where you've been – oh, you naughty, naughty boy, how could you frighten me so?' And she sank down on to the oak bench that stood in the hall and sat there limply, looking very pale and shaken.

'I've just been out and about, Mum,' Sam said, utterly bewildered: he had played truant on other occasions, *and* been discovered, too, but his mother had never reacted like this!

Rose was standing in the doorway of the sitting-room. She was white-faced and wide-eyed. 'Auntie and me – we thought the wolf had got you,' she said.

'Wolf?' Sam looked from his cousin to his mother. Were they both mad? Or was he dreaming it all, was he in the middle of a nightmare? He pinched himself hard and yelped with the pain. 'Wolf?' he repeated.

'Didn't you know?' Rose cried.

'Oh Sam – Sam, you'll be the death of me,' his mother gasped, clapping her hand to her forehead and going whiter still, so that Rose went flying for a glass of water and Sam took her cold hands and rubbed them between his own warm, grubby ones.

'What's it all about?' he demanded, when Mrs Peach had drunk a little water and the colour had returned to her face.

Neither Mrs Peach nor Rose were exactly coherent, but Sam managed to piece the story together. The big dog wolf they had teased in the menagerie had got loose – no one knew how; his absence had been discovered in the middle of the afternoon at feeding time and the alarm had gone out; the children had been sent home early from school and told to stay indoors; the farmers had fetched in their cattle and as many hill sheep as they could round up before darkness fell.

'And of course we thought the wolf had got *you*,' Rose said excitedly. 'Jumped on you somewhere and torn your throat clean out!'

Mrs Peach blanched. 'That's enough, Rose! Sam – there's some tea left on the kitchen table.' She had slipped into a coat and was tying a scarf round her head. 'I won't be long,' she said.

'Where you going, Mum?'

'Just down the road to Mrs Mountjoy's. Your father's there and he'll want to know you're safe. He's sitting with that poor woman – her little boy's not back yet. She must be half-crazed by now, poor soul . . .'

Sam could not speak. He opened his mouth but all that came out was a hoarse squawk that was drowned in the slam of the front door. He stood silent for a minute, listening to the sound of his mother's feet going away down the hill; she had a metal tip on one heel and not on the other. Then he turned to Rose.

'I got to warn Abe,' he said.

It was a very brave thing Sam did then – brave and quite unnecessary, as brave things often are. All he really need have done was to go into the street and call out to one of the men that Abe Tanner and Percy Mountjoy were probably in Gibbet Wood and then he could have gone back indoors and stayed safely, by the fire. Of course he would have had to explain how he knew Percy was there, and there would have been trouble about that later on, but trouble was nothing beside two boys' lives . . .

But Sam did not stop to work this out. The thought did cross his mind that he might run and fetch his father, but he dismissed it: his father was with Mrs Mountjoy and Sam could not face Mrs Mountjoy just now. And even if he could get his father alone, he would have to explain so much, and explanations took up precious time.... No, there was only one thing to do. He must go and find Abe and Percy himself. And he must go at once.

Rose tried to stop him. Mrs Peach had put the dogs in the kitchen and locked the back door; while Sam stood on a stool to try and pull back the rusty, top bolt, Rose hovered below him, begging him not to go.

'You'll be killed Sam – oh, please don't go – what'll I say to Auntie? Well, if you *will* go, let me come too?' Sam shook his head sternly and she sighed. 'Oh, all right then – but take *something* ...'

As Sam got the door open and the cold air breathed into the kitchen, Rose darted at the table drawer and took out the sharp knife Mrs Peach used for cutting the dogs' meat. 'Take this,' she said. 'If the wolf comes at you, you got to get underneath him and slit his throat. I read a book about a man who did that, and there was a picture showing you.' She crouched in the middle of the kitchen floor, the knife point upwards. 'He was a Canadian trapper,' she said.

"I'll cut myself, more like," Sam said, but the idea took his fancy: he made a few passes in the air with the knife, cutting up an imaginary foe, before wrapping the blade in a piece of sacking and sticking it in his belt.

'Take one of the dogs too, take Tarquin,' Rose said. 'Auntie says Salukis used to hunt wolves in the olden days.'

'Not *these* Salukis,' Sam said contemptuously. 'Why – Tarquin's the most awful coward. He ran away from a Pekinese the other day! Anyway, Mum'ud never forgive me if anything happened to him ...'

Rose shivered. 'I don't want to stay behind on my own.'

'Lock the door, you'll be O.K.,' Sam ordered her. He was all swagger and courage at this moment because it suddenly seemed that what he was about to embark upon was just another of the daring adventures that took place almost hourly in his imagination. It was not until Rose had shut the door behind him and he heard the bolt creak into place, that he realized *this* adventure was real.

As Mrs Peach reached the Mountjoy house, she met her husband coming out. 'Percy's back,' he told her, 'walked in half an hour ago, calm as you please.'

'Where has he been? What did he say? Is he hurt?'

'Heaven only knows where he's been. He's not had a chance to say much yet – his mother's done all the talking so far. And he's not hurt, though his mother's making more of a fuss about a bit of a cut on one finger than I'd have thought possible if he'd broken both legs!'

His tone was rather less sympathetic than it had ever been before when speaking of Mrs Mountjoy.

'Sam's safe home too,' Mrs Peach said.

'Good.' Mr Peach glanced at her. 'You really were worried about him, weren't you?' A faint sense of shame stirred in him suddenly and he steered her into the Fisherman's Rest and made her sit down by the welcoming fire to drink a glass of brandy. 'Mind you, I was beginning to get a bit worried about him myself,' he admitted. 'Miss Pennyfather looked in on Mrs Mountjoy to see if Percy was back – and she said Sam hadn't been at school today.'

Mrs Peach frowned. 'Rose didn't say anything.'

'She wouldn't. They're thick as thieves,' Mr Peach said. 'I'll have to have a word with our young man, soon as I get back.'

But he was in no particular hurry. The public house was

full. Castle Stoke was a sleepy place where there was not much to talk about from one year's end to the other; the escaped wolf provided a rare topic of conversation which everyone was enjoying to the full. Most of the men had been out with guns during the early evening but no one had caught even a glimpse of the wolf. The general opinion was that it must have made its way up to the wilder hill country to the west of Castle Stoke – where, if it took a sheep or two before it was shot, at least they wouldn't be local sheep. The atmosphere in the cosy little bar was one of excitement, almost of festivity, and it was a good thirty minutes before Mr and Mrs Peach left it, and walked home to 'have a word' with Sam.

But of course, there was no Sam there. Only Rose, waiting for them in the hall, hunched up on the bottom stair as if she had a stomach ache. As soon as she saw Sam's parents, she burst into tears. Mrs Peach gave a shocked exclamation and sank to her knees beside the weeping child. At first, Rose only shook her head when she was questioned but in the end they coaxed the story out of her.

'Sam's gone to warn Abe and Percy?' Mrs Peach repeated in astonishment. 'But Percy's home now – did Sam think he was with Abe? He couldn't have been – Sam said *he'd* gone off for a visit with old Mrs Tanner . . .'

'That was part of the plan,' Rose said, miserably. Wild horses would not have dragged the story from her in the ordinary way, but now Sam was in danger there seemed nothing else to do. Mr and Mrs Peach listened in silence. 'They did it for me, really,' said poor Rose at the end. 'I was homesick one night and Abe said if we could get the ransom money I could fly off to America.' She looked at Mrs Peach. 'I wanted to come back again, but I wanted to see them just once. . . .' She gave a little sigh. 'Course, we never did get around to asking for the money,' she said.

Mrs Peach put an arm round her. 'It was rather an unkind thing to do wasn't it?' she said softly. 'Poor Mrs Mountjoy – how could you let her suffer so?' She looked up at her husband, sudden horror dawning in her eyes. 'Whatever will she say when she knows?'

'We'll cross that bridge when we come to it,' Mr Peach said. 'We've got other things to worry about now. I'd better go and find Sam.'

Mrs Peach jumped up, strode to the end of the hall and opened the kitchen door. 'Tarquin, Hero . . .' she shouted, and the great dogs got up from the warm rug, yawning and stretching themselves.

'You're not going to exercise the dogs. Not *now*?' Mr Peach said in an awed voice.

Mrs Peach's eyes shone. 'I'm taking them with me – after Sam.' She seized Sam's raincoat from the peg in the hall and gave it to the dogs to smell. 'Go fetch, go fetch . . . .' she cried, and ran through the kitchen to open the back door.

It was a cold, still night with millions of frosty stars high in the velvet canopy of sky, where a pale moon rode full and clear of cloud. The earth lay hushed and ghostly under its light. Trees, bushes, even blades of grass stood out with startling distinctness; in contrast, all shadows were blacker than usual, hiding heaven knew what horror. Sam tried not to look at them, fixing his gaze straight ahead and stepping lightly as he could on the squeaky grass. At first, he was able to keep in the middle of the fields, away from the dangerous shadows, but Gibbet Wood drew closer and closer, until it loomed up in front of him like a dark and menacing wall. Sam almost came to a halt when he reached the outer trees; his feet began to drag as if there were weights in his shoes and his heart beat fast and high in his throat.

He pushed his way through the first brambles, refusing to look to either side or behind him. There were so many things in a wood that might move, or seem to move. Every twig that snapped beneath his feet rang out terrifyingly loud in the stillness. Once or twice he called 'Abe, Percy ...' in a weak, quavery voice, but no one answered. When he reached the gibbet and found the clearing empty, he was so disappointed that painful sobs choked his throat and made his eyes and nose water.

He stood for a minute, rubbing his knuckles in his eyes and snivelling before he pressed on, desperately frightened now, clawing at the wet branches that tore his face and hair, trampling down the tangly briars beneath his feet. It couldn't be long now – surely, this was the place where they had found the best patch of puff-balls this afternoon? There was the tree stump Abe had sat upon! He recognized it with a surge of gratitude and rushed on, through the thinning trees, until he stood at the far edge of Gibbet Wood and the Bent Hill rose above him, grey in the moonlight.

He began to run now, exultantly leaping patches of heather and dying wimberries, suddenly hardly frightened at all now he was safely out of the wood – indeed, as he reached the top of the first bluff, his fear began to seem stupid and childish. What had he been afraid of after all? An old, mangy wolf? He burst out laughing, ran down a little hollow and up the next bluff, carolling at the top of his voice, 'Who's afraid of the big, bad wolf, the big, bad wolf, the big, bad wolf ...'

He was still singing as he breasted the last rise before the old mine and started to run down the slope towards the shack. Then the words faded on his lips. The shack was empty and dark – but it was not its deserted look that silenced him.

Something was lying in front of the shack, its head arched back.

It was Mrs Tanner's goat, and it was quite dead. The front of its throat had been completely torn away.

CHAPTER FIFTEEN

SAM bent to feel the dark, sticky blood on the animal's throat and recoiled, shuddering, before his fingers touched it. Fearfully, he looked round him. No Abe, no Percy, no old, white horse. The hollow lay still and drained of colour in the moonlight; a sleepy chuckling from the closed fowl house was the only sign that there was anything alive here.

Except the wolf, perhaps. He *had* been here, certainly – the dead goat was proof of it. Was he still here, behind one of the shacks perhaps, watching Sam? Sam whipped round, his heart like a pebble in his mouth, but there was nothing behind him except the rise of the bluff, silver-pale against the dark sky.

Where was Abe? Sam listened, straining his ears as if the quiet night could answer him. Then he crept to the door of the shack. It stood half open; there was no light inside except the little glow from the fire which was hissing damply, a kettle steaming on the black hob.

Sam let out a long sigh. Abe must have been here very recently: if he had been away long, the fire would have burned through. He must have sent Percy home and come back alone to make his supper. The goat could not have been dead then – if it had been, Abe would have been too distracted to put on that kettle and make up the fire. No – he had come back to find everything in order; he had milked the goat, shut up the hens and gone indoors for the night.

What had disturbed him? That was easy enough: the goat would not have died silently and the horse would have let out a terrific whinnying if there was a wolf about. The horse – the white horse! Sam gasped and flew to the place where the iron bar that tethered her had been driven into the ground. He found it gone – pulled clean out – and dark marks on the turf where it had been dragged along. Sam crouched beside the jagged hole. A tethered goat, a tethered horse – both easy game for a hungry wolf! The wolf must have killed the goat first and the white horse, driven frantic, had careered round and round at the end of her rope until she tore the iron bar from the ground. Where had she gone? Had Abe gone after her? Of course he had – he would never think of his own skin if his beloved mare was in danger. Had the wolf got him too, or was it stalking him – and if so, where? Through Gibbet Wood or along the grey ridges of the Bent Hill?

Sam leapt to his feet. He had come all at once to a desperate decision – at least, it was desperate for him. He must get help. And the only help that lay within easy distance was Farmer John ...

Sam knew where he lived, of course, in a small, red farmhouse on the quarry side of Gibbet Wood, looking down over cornfields to the sleek, sleepy valley. It was an isolated house, there was no proper road to it, only a rutted cart track, and no telephone, but Farmer John preferred it that way. He lived alone with no woman to trouble him and no hired help either; milking his own cows, ploughing his own fields, keeping himself to himself and becoming, over the years, a terrifying legend to the boys of the village.

Sam had been near the farmhouse once. He had made an expedition with a friend, one October day a year ago. They had not dared go near the yard where the hum of the milking machine told them Farmer John was safely occupied, but had contented themselves with peering through the thick hedge that surrounded the small garden at the back.

There were vegetables in the garden but no flowers; the back windows of the house were uncurtained and looked like dead eyes. They had done nothing but look. An apple tree dropped its fruit their side of the hedge but they did not touch it: Farmer John's apples would kill you. Nor did they trespass in the garden: any boy who ventured further than the hedge was a dead boy, sure as fate.

To knock up Farmer John, then, was the bravest thing Sam did that night. Perhaps it was even the bravest thing he was ever to do, in his whole life. He was frightened, of course – who wouldn't be frightened if they were deliberately walking into an ogre's den – but in spite of his fear he did not waste a minute. He picked up his heels and flew. He ran as fast as he could, down hill, round the wood, and arrived, panting, in Farmer John's yard.

A dog in one of the outhouses began a wild barking and rattling as it flung itself the length of its chain. Sam longed to turn and run back, but he forced himself to advance across the yard, past the log pile and the manure heap, to Farmer John's door. He banged once then leaned, trembling, against the wall.

Inside the house there was a shuffling of feet and then a squeaky drawing of bolts. The door opened with a jerk and a short, fat, bearded man stood there, holding a Tilly lamp. He wore a striped shirt fastened at the collarless neck with a brass stud, cord breeches and thick socks on his unshod feet.

Sam stared at this very ordinary farmer. 'Are you Farmer John?'

'No one else, far as I know.' The man grinned, displaying, not a sabre-sharp fang but an unremarkable set of slightly yellow teeth.

'Oh,' Sam said, 'I thought . . .' He stopped. It was hardly polite to say what he had thought.

Farmer John held the Tilly lamp high. 'What's the matter, boy? You look just about done in.'

Sam explained as quickly as he could. Farmer John nodded. 'Abe . . .' he said. 'That'll be Jess Tanner's boy? Wait on a minute . . .'

He disappeared into the house and emerged a minute later with his boots on and a gun in the crook of his arm. He went across the yard without a word. Sam followed like a dog at his heels.

Farmer John trudged up the Bent Hill, head down, short, fat legs moving like pistons. Sam, running behind, was beginning to think he could keep up no longer, when Farmer John halted suddenly.

'Hard going?' he asked.

Sam nodded; he couldn't speak. Farmer John held out his hand, and, after a second's hesitation, Sam took it. It was like being held by an iron claw.

'I reckon th'old mare'll make for the quarry,' Farmer John said. 'I seen her there more than once – chances are, she'll make for a place she knows.'

They took a short cut through the fringe of Gibbet Wood. 'Been here before?' Farmer John asked. 'Or you scared of the Headless Hunter?'

Sam's breath was coming easier now. 'You ever seen him?' he asked timidly. 'Abe did, once.'

Farmer John chuckled, a warm, deep rumble in his beard. 'All I know is, he keeps boys away from my young pheasants. A wood's got to be kept quiet for pheasants. For other young things, too. Look over there . . .' He gestured across a clearing and Sam's heart thumped – had he seen the wolf? But all Farmer John said was, 'See that bank? I saw a pair of young badgers playing there last spring. Playing in the moonlight pretty as you please.'

'Did you shoot them?'

'Shoot them? What for?' Farmer John looked down at Sam. 'You been looking at my gibbet, have you?'

'You chased Abe and me off,' Sam said boldly.

Farmer John chuckled again. 'Give you a fright, did I? Well – it didn't put young Abe off.' He paused. 'Did the boots fit?' he asked abruptly.

'Boots?' Sam was bewildered.

'Boots I said. Never mind. About the gibbet – well, I got that old badger in my fowl run. He got in one night, making a fair old to-do – fetched me out of my warm bed he did, and I went along with my gun. But I wouldn't'a shot him otherwise, I got too much respect for th'old badger. He keeps hisself to hisself most of the time – minds his own business, and that's a good thing. In humans too, let me tell you.'

All the time he was talking, they were moving at a good, steady pace. They came out of the wood near the quarry. The Bent Hill sloped upwards in front of them to the lonely summit, frosted and desolate. There was nothing in sight: no boy, no horse.

'But they're not *here*,' Sam cried, shocked by the magnitude of this disappointment. He had trusted Farmer John so implicitly that he had given up worrying; he had really expected to find Abe waiting for them on the hill, as if at some prearranged rendezvous. Now Farmer John had turned out to be wrong, all Sam's anxiety returned and weighed on him like lead. Where was Abe? Would they ever find him now? 'Abe, Abe,' he called frantically, wrenching his hand out of Farmer John's in his despair and running aimlessly forward. 'Abe, Abe . . .' His voice choked with sobs.

'Hush a minute.' Farmer John's hand closed on his shoulder so hard that it almost threw him to the ground. 'Steady, now . . .'

They stood, listening. From the direction of the quarry came a faint, answering cry.

Farmer John loosed Sam at once and lumbered forward. Sam tripped, fell, got up again and flew after him like the wind. They reached the edge of the quarry together, and looked down.

Below them, the old mare lay on her side on the floor of the quarry, and Abe knelt beside her.

'She must have run over the edge,' Farmer John said, half to himself, half to Sam, and, hearing his voice, Abe looked up. As he got to his feet, the mare lifted her head.

'Her legs's broke,' Abe said. His voice echoed from the hollow sides of the quarry.

'All right, lad, I'm coming down,' Farmer John said. He turned to Sam. 'Where's the best way.'

'Other side,' Sam told him. 'That's where we . . .' The words dried in his throat as he looked where his finger was pointing. Down the sloping side, a grey shape was moving; as Sam watched, it sprang lightly on to the quarry floor.

The horse gave a terrified neigh and tried to struggle up. Abe screamed – with rage, not fear – and, picking up a loose stone, flung it at the wolf. The wolf halted, one paw in the air like a waiting dog. Farmer John jerked his gun to his shoulder. The wolf rumbled in its throat, and sprang.

The bullet caught him mid-spring and he crumpled. 'Stay there,' Farmer John ordered Sam, and began to slide clumsily down the side of the quarry, his gun slung from his shoulder. He went to the wolf, moved its body with his foot and left it. Sam saw him go up to Abe; together, they looked down at the white horse.

Farmer John was talking. Sam could not hear what he was saying, but he heard Abe cry out once, and Farmer John put a hand on his shoulder. Abe went down on his knees by the mare and put his arms round her neck; he seemed to be whispering in her ear. Then he stood up and walked away. He stood with his face to the wall of the quarry, hands dangling limply at his sides. Farmer John's gun cracked once more. The white mare jerked, and lay still.

There was deep silence. Sam could hear every creak of Farmer John's boots as he walked over to Abe. But before he reached him, Abe leapt for the side of the quarry and went up like a fly. Sam ran to meet him at the top but Abe went past him as if he didn't exist. His face was a white mask. He ran in great leaps down the hill and disappeared into Gibbet Wood.

Farmer John puffed wearily up to Sam. 'Where'd he go?' he asked shortly.

Sam pointed to the wood. 'Shall we go after him?'

Farmer John shook his head. 'There's some things best left ...' He took out his pipe and began to fill it slowly. 'No good to go after him,' he said. 'Grief heals best left alone. Especially with *that* one I shouldn't wonder. D'you see much of him?'

'I'm his best friend.'

'Only friend, more like,' Farmer John said.

'Oh no – Rose is his friend, too,' Sam said, and was beginning to explain about Rose when Farmer John held up his hand, hushing him.

'Listen,' he said, and Sam heard a sound, distant at first and then coming nearer – a sound to make the blood run cold: the sound of hunting dogs in full cry. It was coming from the direction of the Tanner's shack. Farmer John put his unlit pipe in his pocket and set off at a great pace across the hill.

Though Sam and Farmer John made good speed, Mr and Mrs Peach reached the shack first – and Mrs Tanner had got there before any of them.

When they emerged from Gibbet Wood, Sam's parents had seen her, an erect, dark figure toiling upwards through the heather.

'It's Mrs Tanner,' Mr Peach said. 'Call the dogs off . . .'

But it was too late. The four great dogs had been running silently ahead of them, nose to ground, sniffing for Sam's scent; now, suddenly, they lifted their heads and sprang forward, howling.

'Tarquin, Hero – *Hero*,' Mrs Peach cried, but they paid no heed. Though they had lost Sam's scent, they had found another – the strange, rank scent of the wolf. Wild with excitement, they bounded across the heather, making straight for Mrs Tanner.

'Oh God,' Mrs Peach moaned. 'She's in their way – they'll run her down . . .'

Then something strange and wonderful happened. When the dogs were almost upon her, Mrs Tanner turned. Whether she spoke or not, no one was near enough to know, but the dogs checked suddenly in mid-bound – as if they had hurtled up against an invisible fence. Their howling ceased; they crouched on their bellies and crept round Mrs Tanner, forming a semi-circle. Then they lay down, their heads raised and looking at her. They did not move, neither when Sam's parents panted up, nor when Sam himself breasted the brow of the hill with Farmer John. They were still as if they had been turned to stone, and before them Mrs Tanner stood, still as stone herself, her blind face marble-pale in the moonlight.

No one spoke for a moment. The spell that held the dogs seemed to hold them all. Then Mr Peach cleared his throat and the old woman turned her head questioningly towards him.

'Who are you?' she asked. 'Why has there been trouble here?'

Before Sam had time to wonder how she knew, Farmer John stepped forward. 'The trouble's over, Jess,' he said. 'But you've lost your goat and your boy's lost his horse – I had to shoot her, both her forelegs were broken.'

Most women would have cried out at this: they would have said 'Oh dear, how dreadful!' or 'However did it happen?' But Mrs Tanner merely nodded, slowly, and said, 'Where is he?'

'Abe? In the wood. No – don't whistle him up, Jess.' Farmer John looked round at Sam, at his parents, at the waiting dogs, and grinned suddenly. 'He'll hardly come while this reception committee's around. Go inside, Jess, and sit by the fire. I'll set the lamp in the window. He'll come once he knows his Gran's home and waiting.'

CHAPTER SIXTEEN

To his cousin Rose, even to his parents, Sam was the hero of the hour. Once home, a blazing fire was stoked up and they all sat round it, with no mention of bedtime, while he told his story from first to last, adding a few extra incidents for good measure: How he had first caught sight of the wolf in Gibbet Wood and stalked it with his hunting knife; how, having lost it, he had come up to the old mine while the savage creature was actually killing the goat. He gave a blood-curdling imitation of the noise the goat had made which made Rose gasp and turn pale. ''Course, soon as I got up to it, it ran off,' he said, thinking how much better a story it would have made if he could have claimed that he had fallen upon the wolf then and there and killed it with his knife, but realizing, regretfully, that he had to fit his story in to the facts that were already known. He made as much as he could of his journey down to Farmer John and the desperate haste with which they had gone to Abe's rescue, emphasizing his own part as much as he decently could: Farmer John had shot the wolf but it had been Sam who saw it first – if he had not, it might have killed Abe, as it had killed the goat.

If his parents were less convinced than Rose of all the details of Sam's heroic performance, they gave no sign of it. When Sam had finished, Mr Peach cleared his throat, adjusted his spectacles and said, 'You did very well, my boy. I'm proud of you.' He paused, his eyes fixed on the wall above Sam's head, and added, casually, 'It's just as well young Percy was safe home by then.'

He said no more, but Sam was suddenly uneasy. He glanced at Rose. She hung her head.

'I *had* to tell them, Sam,' she whispered, creeping into Sam's room later on, when they were both supposed to be in bed and asleep. She looked, and sounded, so miserable that Sam hadn't the heart to be cross with her; he kissed her and said, magnanimously, that he dared say he would have done the same in her place. 'But why didn't they say something about it?' he asked in a wondering voice. 'I should've thought they'd have been ever so angry, don't you think it's funny?'

'Perhaps they were so glad you were safe that they didn't feel angry.'

Sam thought about this for a minute. 'I'd have thought they'd have *said* something, just the same.'

'Perhaps they thought they'd wait till tomorrow,' was all Rose could say – a suggestion that did nothing to make Sam sleep easier. He tossed and turned all night, the memory of his exciting adventure subdued by anxiety. By tomorrow, his father would have got used to the fact that he was alive and well. What would happen then?

To Sam's utter amazement, nothing happened at all. He came down to breakfast looking pale and tired and Mrs Peach said he must stay home from school to recover from his ordeal. He mooned about the house all day, outwardly languid and bored and inwardly trembling, waiting for the storm to break. But the day passed and no mention was made of the kidnapping. Sam went to bed and spent another restless night: looking at his exhausted face the next morning, his mother insisted that a further day's rest was called for, sent Rose to school with a note for Miss Penny-father, and tucked Sam up on the sofa by the fire.

Mid-morning, his father came in for coffee. He had a distinctly cheerful air. Spooning sugar into his cup and reaching out for the ginger biscuits, he announced, casually, that he had happened to meet Mrs Mountjoy up the Town and been delighted to hear that young Percy was none the worse for his adventure. 'Apparently he slept out in the wood all that night,' he said. He looked straight at Sam and Sam thought he winked, but the sunlight was pouring straight into the room and dazzling his eyes so that he couldn't be sure.

From that moment, Sam began to recover. He wasted no time on wondering whether his father had disbelieved Rose's story or whether he had simply, and for some incomprehensible reason, decided to ignore it: either way, it was clear Sam had been reprieved. By lunch time he had recovered his appetite so completely that he ate three helpings of steak and kidney pie and two of Queen Pudding. Mrs Peach decided that fresh air was all that was needed to complete his cure and sent him off to meet Rose out of school.

He met Mrs Mountjoy as she was going into her house with Percy. Sam's heart thumped at the sight of her, but she smiled at him graciously and said she had heard he had been a very, very brave little boy. If Sam had been more responsive, she might have said more, but he only hung his head and peered nervously sidelong at Percy, who was wearing a smart new grey flannel suit and a white shirt with a red bow tie. Percy's face was inscrutable: he returned Sam's look blankly, as if he had never seen him before, but as soon as Mrs Mountjoy had turned to open her front door he darted after Sam and caught him by the sleeve.

'I've got to go to school tomorrow,' he gabbled, pink beneath his freckles. 'Tell Abe . . .'

'*Ssh,*' Sam whispered urgently, glancing over his shoulder at Mrs Mountjoy, but she was out of earshot, waiting for Percy at the top of the steps and smiling benevolently.

Percy pulled a face. 'Don't take any notice of *her*. Tell Abe I'll see him next holidays and give him this.' He held out a marble – a beautiful, big marble, deep orange in colour and with whorls of black and purple. 'And tell him I had a lovely time,' he said.

'I'll tell him soon as I see him,' Sam said.

But he did not see Abe. He did not appear at school and as for ten days the weather was bad, with high winds and driving rain, Rose and Sam felt disinclined to go up to the old mine to look for him.

On Saturday morning they woke to find the weather had changed. There was still a wind, but the sun was shining and the sky was clear. It was very cold. 'The year's turning,' Mrs Peach said, looking out of the kitchen window at the frost and the tall dahlias, blackened on their stakes.

Rose and Sam put sandwiches in their pockets in case they got hungry mid-morning.

'Shall we go up through Gibbet Wood?' Rose asked.

'If you like ...' A little to his surprise, Sam found he did not care much, one way or the other. The wood no longer drew him, now he knew there was nothing frightening about it. 'It's just an old wood,' he said, with a fleeting sense of regret for the days when the mere mention of the place had been enough to send a shiver down his spine.

'It's the shortest way to the mine,' Rose said sensibly, and so they made up towards it, along the boundary of the cob nut field, keeping in the lee of the hedge because the wind was keen. On the other side of the hedge a tractor was chugging. 'That'll be Farmer John ploughing,' Sam said, and they stopped at the gate to look.

But it wasn't Farmer John. Abe sat on the tractor seat, a sack draped over his shoulders and a cloth cap perched sideways on his ragged hair. His face wore a set, determined expression as he negotiated the difficult turn at the top of the field and bore down towards them. Though they waved and shouted, he didn't stop – indeed, except for one brief, sideways glance, he ignored them altogether. He drove past, on down to the bottom of the field, the brown earth furling away from the plough and the gulls flying behind him. 'He's going a bit crooked,' Sam said.

Rose gave him a scornful look. 'Jealous,' she said.

Abe turned at the bottom of the field and drove back towards them. In spite of the noise of the tractor they could hear him whistling.

'Abe,' Rose called, and this time he did stop, halting the tractor by the gate. He got down from his perch and came towards them, hitching at his trousers with a self-conscious swagger. 'I'm givin' Farmer John a hand to git his ploughin' done,' he announced casually.

'Are you working for him, then?' Rose asked. 'Aren't you coming back to school?'

Abe shrugged his shoulders. 'Reckon they'll be after me if I don't. I ain't old enough to leave yet, worse luck. Farmer John says when I do leave, I c'n work for him reg'lar. Now I'm jus' obligin' him, like.' While he spoke, he stared over their heads. He seemed shy, Sam began to feel shy too, he wasn't sure why.

He said diffidently, 'Percy asked me to tell you he had a lovely time. He said to give you this.'

Abe looked at the marble, rolled it briefly round his grubby palm and then stuffed it in his pocket. 'He gone away, then?'

'Back to his school.' Sam paused. 'He didn't say anything about us – not a thing!'

'D'you think he would, then?' Abe smiled to himself, pushed his cloth cap forward on his head and shot a quick glance at Rose through his tangled fringe. Then he pulled a flask out of his pocket. 'Cold tea,' he said. 'Thirsty work, ploughing.' He set the flask to his lips and took a long, gurgling pull.

'I reckon it was nice of him to keep quiet,' Sam said. Thinking of the two miserable nights he had spent, lying awake and worrying, he felt annoyed with Abe for his careless attitude. 'He could've got us into most awful trouble,' he said reproachfully . 'He could've . . .'

'Oh, he ain't a bad kid.' Abe cut him short, speaking in the airy, condescending tone of someone dismissing a boring subject. He narrowed his eyes and peered up the field. 'That's not a bad bit of ploughin',' he said.

Sam set his lips, determined not to be impressed by this blatant showing-off, but Rose said admiringly, 'I think it's lovely, I bet Farmer John couldn't do it any better.'

'I bet *I* could do just as good,' Sam muttered, but this sounded unconvincing even to himself, and Abe did not bother to reply. He merely nodded and said, 'Well, I best git on,' and his manner, friendly but distant, suddenly seemed to Sam to open up a gulf between them: on the one side there was Abe, doing a grown man's work – he might boast but he had something to boast about – while on the other all poor Sam could do was to stand and watch him enviously, a kid, like Percy . . .

Rose's eyes were fixed on Abe. 'Don't go just yet,' she begged him. 'I mayn't see you again, not for a long time, anyway. My parents are coming soon. Auntie wrote and said I was missing them and they sent a telegram . . .'

Abe said quickly, 'They'll tek you away, then?'

Rose nodded. 'I wish I wasn't going, really. I like it here. I liked being in the gang and everything, I shan't ever forget it. Auntie says I can come back though, next year if I like – we'll make another gang, then, shall we?'

Abe's face had a queer, set look so that it was impossible to tell what he was thinking. He looked down at his muddy boots and it seemed a long time before he said, 'Oh, you won't want to play kid's games next year.' He gave a sudden, loud guffaw that made the resting gulls fly up from the turned earth. 'You'll be a young lady,' he said.

Rose went pink. 'Don't be silly.'

Abe looked at her, frowning. 'T'aint silly. Things'll be different, you'll see.'

'D'you mean because of Whitey? Because we can't be the White Horse Gang any more?' She put her hand on Abe's arm. 'I'm sorry about Whitey, Eba.'

'T'aint just that *she's* dead,' Abe said, frowning harder than ever. He swallowed and looked as if there was something he wanted to say but did not see how to. 'It's jus' that things is always different,' he managed finally. 'I mean t'was fine, bein' a gang an' all, but t'won't be the same next year, t'won't be the same ever again.'

Rose was watching his face. She said slowly, 'You mean we shan't be the same? You mean we'll feel different?'

'*I* shan't feel no different,' Sam said stoutly. He thought Abe and Rose were being extraordinarily stupid. Why – he was quite sure he would never change from the person he was at this moment, nor want to do different things from the things he wanted to do now.

'Mebbe you won't then, you're just a kid yet,' Abe said.

Though he hadn't spoken unkindly, Sam doubled his fists, hatred suddenly burning up inside him. How dare Abe called him a kid after all that had happened: hadn't he rescued him from the wolf, hadn't he saved his life? He didn't want to be thanked but Abe might at least be polite, not speak to him in that horrible, condescending way ...

Abe looked at Sam's furious, red face, and then, thought-

154

fully, at the tractor. Suddenly his face split into a huge, happy grin.

''F I start her up, would you like a go?'' he asked.

A glorious hour, and several rather wavy furrows later, they said good-bye at the gate. Abe sat on the top rung, watching them go, waving whenever they turned round. The fine morning was over and the clouds were coming up: when Sam and Rose looked back at Abe he seemed a small, rather lonely figure in the darkening landscape and they felt a sudden, disturbing sadness – almost, Sam thought, as if they were saying good-bye to him for ever. But of course that was nonsense: Abe would always be there. If they liked, they could go to see him tomorrow, and the next day and the next.... Halfway down the hill the sadness had begun to lift and by the time they reached the Peach field where the Christmas trees were planted, it had disappeared altogether. Shouting and laughing, they raced each other home.

THE PRIME MINISTER'S BRAIN
Gillian Cross

The fiendish Demon Headmaster plans to gain control of No. 10 Downing Street and lure the Prime Minister into his evil clutches.

JASON BODGER AND THE PRIORY GHOST
Gene Kemp

A ghost story, both funny and exciting, about Jason, the bane of every teacher's life, who is pursued by the ghost of a little nun from the twelfth century!

HALFWAY ACROSS THE GALAXY AND TURN LEFT
Robin Klein

A humorous account of what happens to a family banished from their planet Zygron, when they have to spend a period of exile on Earth.

TOM TIDDLER'S GROUND
John Rowe Townsend

Vic and Brain are given an old rowing boat which leads to the unravelling of a mystery and a happy reunion of two friends. An exciting adventure story.

JELLYBEAN
Tessa Duder

A sensitive modern novel about Geraldine, alias 'Jellybean', who leads a rather solitary life as the only child of a single parent. She's tired of having to fit in with her mother's busy schedule, but a new friend and a performance of 'The Nutcracker Suite' change everything.

THE PRIESTS OF FERRIS
Maurice Gee

Susan Ferris and her cousin Nick return to the world of O which they had saved from the evil Halfmen, only to find that O is now ruled by cruel and ruthless priests. Can they save the inhabitants of O from tyranny? An action-packed and gripping story by the author of prize-winning THE HALFMEN OF O.

THE SEA IS SINGING
Rosalind Kerven

In her seaside Shetland home, Tess is torn between the plight of the whales and loyalty to her father and his job on the oil rig. A haunting and thought-provoking novel.

BACK HOME
Michelle Magorian

A marvellously gripping story of an irrepressible girl's struggle to adjust to a new life. Twelve-year-old Rusty, who had been evacuated to the United States when she was seven, returns to the grey austerity of post-war Britain.

RACSO AND THE RATS OF NIMH

Jane Leslie Conly

When fieldmouse Timothy Frisby rescues young Racso, the city rat, from drowning it's the beginning of a friendship and an adventure. The two are caught up in the struggle of the Rats of NIMH to save their home from destruction. A powerful sequel to MRS FRISBY AND THE RATS OF NIMH.

NICOBOBINUS

Terry Jones

Nicobobinus and his friend, Rosie, find themselves in all sorts of intriguing adventures when they set out to find the Land of the Dragons long ago. Stunningly illustrated by Michael Foreman.

FRYING AS USUAL

Joan Lingard

When Mr Francetti breaks his leg it looks as if his fish restaurant will have to close so Tony, Rosita and Paula decide to keep things going.

DRIFT

William Mayne

A thrilling adventure of a young boy and an Indian girl, stranded on a frozen floating island in the North American wilderness.